TOM SWIFT AND HIS JETMARINE

THE NEW TOM SWIFT JR. ADVENTURES
BY VICTOR APPLETON II

TOM SWIFT AND HIS FLYING LAB
TOM SWIFT AND HIS JETMARINE
TOM SWIFT AND HIS ROCKET SHIP
TOM SWIFT AND HIS GIANT ROBOT
TOM SWIFT AND HIS ATOMIC EARTH BLASTER
TOM SWIFT AND HIS OUTPOST IN SPACE

"I was sitting on deck when everyone blacked out!"

THE NEW TOM SWIFT JR. ADVENTURES

TOM SWIFT

AND HIS JETMARINE

BY VICTOR APPLETON II

ILLUSTRATED BY GRAHAM KAYE

GROSSET & DUNLAP

NEW YORK PUBLISHERS

CONTENTS

CONTENTS

ILLUSTRATIONS

TOM SWIFT AND HIS JETMARINE

CHAPTER 1

WING-TIP ESCAPE

THE RED SIGNAL flashed on the giant control board of the Swifts' private TV network. A blond youth of eighteen with deep-set blue eyes unhooked his long legs from the rungs of a stool and swung away from a drawing board to which was tacked the blueprint of a submarine. He flicked on the video-phone.

"What's up?" Tom Swift asked Kane, their Key West telecaster, as the man's face settled into focus on the screen.

"Another Caribbean ship attack, Tom." Walking in front of some palm trees, the telecaster continued, "I'm at Marlin Bay, talking to survivors. I have bad news. A passenger freighter, the *Nantic*, has been sunk. Your uncle is among those missing!"

"Uncle Ned!"

"He's reported lost along with the captain and purser. The rest were picked up in lifeboats." Kane

1

passed the microphone to a stout man who was saying nervously, "—but I really don't know what happened. Neither does anyone else on board. I was sitting on deck reading when—*poof*—everyone blacked out! As I came to, the ship was sinking and I got into one of the lifeboats. A schooner picked us up."

"Did you hear any gunfire, any explosions before the blackout?" Kane asked him.

"No. Nothing but the whistle of an airplane."

"Do you think the missing men might be in other boats that weren't picked up?" Kane questioned.

"It's possible."

A Coast Guard officer stepped into view. He told Kane that survivors of similar attacks on other vessels had also mentioned hearing a plane just before everyone had blacked out.

"In those attacks the robbers took everything of value before the passengers revived," the officer said. "But they didn't sink the ships."

"Kane, I'm signing off," Tom announced, then dashed out of the office.

He leaped into a jeep and drove rapidly toward his father's laboratory. On the way his anxiety for Uncle Ned increased by the minute.

"The news will be a shock to Dad," Tom murmured worriedly.

Ned Newton and Mr. Swift, close friends for years, had worked and fought their way together through countless tight situations. The two men had combined also in the building up of the old Swift Construction Company, a widely known concern which manufactured Mr. Swift's various inventions.

In its many branches throughout the country the company had installed its own TV network. This was used also by the new Swift Enterprises, a gleaming four-mile-square stretch of modern buildings and crisscrossed airstrips where Tom and his father carried on experiments.

At this moment Tom's usual smile of pride in them was absent. His thoughts were centered entirely on the terrible climax to Uncle Ned's business trip to South America.

Arriving at his father's one-story all-glass laboratory, Tom hurried into the building. A secretary stopped his mad dash.

"Your father's not here," she said. "I've been trying to get him at the underground hangar but he doesn't answer. An urgent telephone call from the Navy Department has just come in."

"I'll take it," Tom offered. Picking up the phone, he said, "Hello."

"Is this Mr. Swift?"

"Tom Jr. speaking."

"I see," the voice continued. "This is Admiral Hopkins—Navy Intelligence."

"Yes, sir. Dad's often spoken of you. What can we do for you?"

"Tom, we need the Swifts' scientific help on these Caribbean attacks. Frankly we're baffled by the blackout technique."

The admiral explained that his department had

been unable to figure out by what method persons on the victim ships were knocked unconscious just before the looters came aboard.

"We've proved it's not an inside job," he said, "but that only makes the problem worse. Who are these mysterious raiders, and how can they disappear so quickly after plundering the ships? If we weren't so practical, we could almost believe the attacks were engineered by space pirates!"

Tom chuckled, then became serious. "We'll certainly help you all we can, Admiral Hopkins. Dad and I have a special reason of our own for wanting to clear up this mystery."

This would not be the first mystery Tom had solved. In his Flying Lab he had tracked down a group of clever spies responsible for the kidnaping of several scientists.

When Tom told Admiral Hopkins about Ned Newton, the officer expressed his concern. He said that since the *Nantic* was the first ship to be sunk, his department believed that it might be because something had gone wrong in the attackers' plans.

"It's possible your Uncle Ned might not have blacked out," the admiral suggested.

"Which would mean," Tom added, "that the pirates, fearing he'd guessed their secret blackout method, took him prisoner."

"If it's true, and we can locate Mr. Newton," Admiral Hopkins replied, "it may lead us to the hideout of those devils!"

"Nothing would suit me better than to find them," Tom said.

The conversation ended and he ran from the laboratory. Hopping into the jeep, he sped toward the underground hangar on the Enterprises grounds. Tom beamed his electronic key on the door and watched it inch open.

Down in the vast space below ground, where the *Sky Queen,* the Swifts' Flying Lab, was housed, he found his father and told him the alarming news. Mr. Swift listened intently.

"Ned missing!" he murmured. "Oh, no!" Then he added hopefully, "Tom, you know Ned always was very resourceful. If he's alive, he'll find some way to communicate with us."

"Yes, he could use that miniaturized twenty-meter transmitter and receiver I built inside a pencil and gave him before he went away," Tom said. "I hope the pirates didn't take it from him. Well, if Uncle Ned contacts us, we'll be ready to go to his aid on a minute's notice!"

"We certainly will," Mr. Swift agreed.

"But even if Uncle Ned can't contact us, I'd like to start a search for him, anyway."

"How?" his father asked.

"First, let's take up the *Sky Queen* and scan the general area of the ocean where the *Nantic* was attacked," Tom replied. "It's just possible Uncle Ned may be adrift, instead of being a captive. If that fails, the next step would be to speed up the finishing touches on my new two-man sub and go after those pirates. I don't think they can be taken by a surface vessel."

"You think the pirates may be operating with a

sub?" Mr. Swift questioned. "I thought a plane was involved."

"I believe it's a combination," Tom replied. "A blackout ray is sent by their pilot from a plane, then the pirates board the ship from a sub and loot it."

"Quite a system," Mr. Swift reflected, "and devised by men who won't be easy to capture."

"Dad, suppose I warm up the *Sky Queen* while you phone Mother and the office where we're going," Tom suggested.

"All right, son."

Twenty minutes later the huge atomic-powered, jet-lifted craft took off from the Enterprises' private airfield. The plane sped toward the Caribbean area. An hour later the search was on—high over the ocean one minute, then so low the *Sky Queen* was barely above the waves. It did not miss an inch of the territory on which a lifeboat from the *Nantic* might be bobbing.

"I guess we must admit defeat, Tom," Mr. Swift announced finally. "Turn her toward home and let's hope that Ned is still alive."

Not a word was spoken on the return trip until the *Sky Queen* was being berthed at four o'clock. Then Tom spoke.

"I feel sure Uncle Ned's being held a prisoner by those pirates, Dad. With my atomic sub I could beat them at their own game."

"You certainly could, Tom," his father agreed. "I feel more hopeful about rescuing Ned already!"

They drove back to Tom's new combination office

and laboratory. Tom's friend Bud Barclay, who had just returned from a month's flying trip, was draped over the arm of a comfortable leather chair, waiting for them.

Bud was a handsome, dark-haired youth with a well-built, supple body. He had worked with Tom at the Enterprises plant for a couple of years. Just now he was watching the radityper, an instrument which picked up and decoded radio messages. At this moment it was beamed on the Caribbean sector.

"Hi, Bud!" Tom greeted him. "Glad you're back." Then, looking at the clock, he said, "I'm supposed to meet Sandy at the Swift Construction airfield about now. How about coming along?"

"Sure, but what's this about Uncle Ned?"

Tom repeated the story and Bud said, "I figured you might be needing me for a search in the Caribbean, so I came here right away."

Tom smiled appreciatively. "Since Dad and I didn't get a clue on our trip down there, maybe you and I will have to go. Sorry you weren't here to search with us."

"I might have known. A fellow would have to be swinging on the Swifts' coattails not to be left behind," Bud remarked, then added seriously, "Tom, we'd better get started to meet Sandy and break the news about Uncle Ned to her."

Sandra Swift, called Sandy by her family and friends, was a year younger than her brother and an excellent pilot. Both Tom Sr. and Tom Jr. had taught her how to fly.

The boys left the laboratory and set off in the jeep for the commercial airfield at the old Swift Construction Company. Part of the plant there manufactured aircraft and test flights were made daily.

"A swell day for flying," Bud remarked. "There's nothing that can beat flying."

"With one exception—my new sub," Tom replied. "I have a lot of faith in the jetmarine and I'm sticking with her until she's ready for action."

"Tell me more about this latest invention of yours, Tom. I'd like to get the full pitch on the jetmarine and help you try it out, since we'll have to wait a while for our rocket trip into space."

Some time before, a huge meteorlike object had plunged into the Swift Enterprises grounds. On the missile's metal side were mathematical symbols. When Tom had deciphered the code he discovered that it contained a message from the inhabitants of another planet. Ever since, he had dreamed of visiting these space beings—but first his newest invention, the jetmarine, must be perfected.

Tom's two-man submarine was to be manufactured and sold eventually as a speed craft for safe ocean travel, especially to distant points such as Africa and Australia. This type of travel would avoid the delays sometimes experienced by surface ships and aircraft during bad weather.

The submarine was to operate on an entirely different principle of propulsion from the standard propeller type. A stream of water forced through special tubes under great pressure would be its means of propulsion.

"A hydraulic jet," Tom explained.

"Give it to me in first-grade science," Bud begged.

Tom laughed. "Remember when we were kids and filled balloons with water, then let go of them? Same kind of propulsion."

"But all I got was a soaking!" Bud remarked. "Go ahead, professor."

The young inventor explained further that the submarine had an atomic pile containing Swiftonium, the radioactive isotope which the Swifts had discovered in South America. In order to protect the occupants of the jetmarine from the deadly radiation, the whole power plant had been encased in a three-inch thickness of Tomasite. This was a strong, durable plastic named after the young inventor and his father. Heat-resistant, it absorbed gamma rays much more efficiently than lead shields which are ordinarily used.

"Sounds terrific," Bud reflected. "Go on."

Tom said that the submarine, except for its transparent nose, was double-hulled.

"As I see it," Bud interrupted, "the construction of this sub is just like sticking a cigar into one end of an egg and leaving a little of it protruding."

"Right. Only the part of the cigar that you can see is as clear as glass," Tom replied. "The nose is molded of transparent Tomasite."

The outer hull was also painted with Tomasite,

to prevent reflection of sound waves. Thus, the jetmarine could not be detected by sonar devices.

"This is wonderful, genius boy," said Bud, grinning. "But you still haven't told me what makes the jetmarine go."

Tom laughed. "I haven't? Well, the intense heat from the atomic pile will create steam to drive a turbine, which in turn will activate a pump. This will force out a jet of sea water so fast that it will cause propulsion.

"What's holding me up now is the speed control," Tom went on. "And also I still haven't a foolproof way of keeping the water intakes from fouling."

"One thing at a time, skipper," Bud pleaded. "Just how do you control the speed?"

"It's regulated by a battery of cadmium rods. They control the rate of fission when they're inserted or withdrawn from the atomic pile. The deeper the rods are inserted into the pile, the less the heat energy. The more the rods are withdrawn, the faster we generate power."

"I'll take a dozen." Bud laughed. "Say, this may be Sandy coming now." He pointed skyward to a black speck growing larger. "That's one of your *Pigeon Specials*, isn't it?"

"Yes. She's demonstrating it to a prospective buyer."

When they arrived at the field, the boys climbed to the observation tower, where the dispatcher told them that Sandy was cleared to land.

"She certainly knows how to handle a ship," Bud

said admiringly as they watched her swing deftly into the air traffic pattern.

"Indeed she does—" Tom started to say when his attention was drawn to a small red plane that was flying in across the field at Sandy's altitude.

"Look!" Bud cried. "That plane's cutting her out!"

"It's Sidney Dansitt's plane," the flight dispatcher said.

He shouted into his mike for Dansitt to stay away, that Sandy's plane had clearance to land first. But the pilot merely increased his speed, held his course, and bore in on the *Pigeon*. Sandy seemed oblivious of the danger.

The three in the observation tower turned colder than the concrete floor and their necks stiffened as they watched helplessly.

"Sandy, look out!" Tom cried.

The next instant, just as it appeared as if the planes might collide, Sandy realized what was happening. She gave her ship full throttle, pulled back hard on the stick, and the little craft shot up.

"Whew!" Bud said. "One more foot and—"

As Dansitt's plane lurched down the runway, Tom was white with anger. The flier's carelessness had nearly cost his sister her life!

"That crazy pilot!" he cried. "I'll wrap his wings around his neck!"

With a bound Tom was out of the control tower. He leaped down the steps and ran up the field toward Dansitt's plane which was taxiing in.

Suddenly a man raced toward the craft from the opposite direction. As it stopped, the door opened and the stranger quickly climbed inside. Tom, running at top speed, was only a dozen yards from the plane.

"What do you mean, coming in—" he cried out, but did not finish.

Without warning Dansitt's plane shot forward, heading straight at Tom!

CHAPTER 2

A BRAZEN DENIAL

AS DANSITT'S PLANE roared toward Tom, Bud Barclay and the dispatcher stared horrified. There was no time for Tom to dodge completely out of the way!

But, as the two watched, he threw himself to the ground. The left wing tip rushed above him, missing his head by inches.

Bud, already out of the tower, rushed to his friend's aid as Dansitt sped by and took off. As the cloud of dust raised by the exhaust cleared, Bud saw to his relief that Tom was struggling to his feet and shaking a fist at the departing plane.

"You're all right?" Bud asked unbelievingly.

Tom coughed violently. "I'm okay," he gasped, slapping the dust from his clothes. "But I sure have a score to settle with Dansitt!"

"I'll say! He tried to kill you! But why?"

"There must be more to this than meets the eye.

13

I never saw or heard of him. But I mean to find out what's going on!"

"Let's go back to the control tower and make him fly in," Bud urged.

The boys had walked only a dozen yards when Tom suddenly stopped and bent down. He picked up a small gleaming object from the runway.

"What did you find?" Bud asked.

"A coin. *Republica Cuba*," Tom read slowly. "Why, it's a Cuban peso." He turned it over. "But look at this!" he exclaimed. "The head of a dog has been embossed over the original design!"

"That's strange," Bud remarked. "Why would anyone want to do that?"

"Beats me," Tom replied, slipping it into his pocket. "I wonder if Sidney Dansitt or his passenger could have dropped it."

Tom threw himself to the ground

Dansitt sped by and took off

Sandy, meanwhile, had landed the *Pigeon Special*. The girl's blue eyes sparkled as she introduced her client, Miss Carlton, and told the boys how lucky she was to have avoided a crack-up.

"It was more than luck," said Miss Carlton, apparently still a bit shaky. "It was quick thinking. If the necessity arises, I hope I can do as well when I fly the *Pigeon*. I've decided to buy one," she added.

As the group walked toward the parking area,

Tom suggested that Bud drive Sandy and Miss Carlton back to Shopton in his car.

"I want to stay here and have a talk with that wild man Dansitt if he comes back," Tom said.

"Okay. And bring me his head on a platter," Bud said, grinning.

When the others had left, Tom returned to the glass-enclosed room of the dispatcher. He heard him say:

"Sidney Dansitt! Calling Sidney Dansitt! You have been ordered by the Air Patrol to return to this field at once. And don't attempt to land without being cleared!"

There was no answer. The dispatcher repeated his message. Still no reply. With a gesture of disgust, he switched off the mike.

"Who is this Dansitt fellow?" Tom asked him.

"He's a graduate science student at the University. A wise guy. I've been told he has no regard whatsoever for other people's rights."

"That's pretty obvious," Tom said. "This is only a semipublic field. Any more stunts like that and he'll be barred from here altogether. Do you know anything else about Dansitt?"

"Not much. He owns the plane he's in. He flies a lot and he's been making several long-distance trips lately." Suddenly the dispatcher pointed and said:

"Here he comes now."

Tom peered out the green-tinted glass windows and spotted Dansitt's plane approaching the field.

"I'm going to talk to him," Tom told the dispatcher.

As Tom left the tower, Dansitt was banking his plane sharply and coming down for a landing without bothering to fly the prescribed traffic pattern.

"A real hotrock!" Tom exclaimed angrily.

Dansitt sped his plane down the runway, then turned to taxi slowly back to the parking apron. Tom stood waiting as Dansitt stepped out. The young inventor was surprised to discover that the pilot was alone.

"What was the idea of that show you put on? You almost killed three people!" Tom cried.

The cocky stranger's thin lips curled into a sneer.

"You didn't get killed, so what are you beefing about?" he asked huffily.

"You saw me in front of your plane," Tom said with mounting anger. "What was the idea of trying to run me down?"

"I almost didn't see you. I—I looked down at the cabin floor for a second," Dansitt replied evasively.

Tom thrust his hand into his pocket and flashed the dog's-head coin in his open palm.

"Were you looking for this?"

Dansitt stared at the coin and started to grab it. Then, changing his mind, he gazed insolently straight into Tom's eyes.

"I never saw that coin before," he said.

Tom pocketed the piece. "Dansitt," he said, "one more exhibition like today's and it will be your last as a pilot!"

Without waiting for any comment from Dansitt, Tom turned on his heel and strode off toward the Swift home. A few minutes later a mechanic pulled up in a jeep and gave the young scientist a lift the rest of the way.

Entering the house, he found his mother and Sandy gravely discussing Uncle Ned's disappearance.

"It's terrible not to have any inkling of what happened to Ned," Mrs. Swift said. "I feel so sorry for Mrs. Newton and Phyllis."

"She'll take it hard," Tom said, thinking of Ned's pretty, dark-haired daughter Phyl, whom he dated.

Sandy interrupted. "Dad's coming into the driveway now. He looks excited. Maybe he has news."

Mr. Swift strode into the house. "We've received word from Ned!" he cried. "Listen to this!"

"Then he's alive!" Mrs. Swift exclaimed in relief. Tom and Sandy shouted joyously.

"Yes, he's alive, but a prisoner," Mr. Swift said. "He must have used that transmitter in the pencil you gave him, Tom. I unscrambled his message on the radityper. It breaks down to:

'Ned Okay Dog Eight Days! Don't Contact.' "

"Have you any idea what 'Dog' means, Dad?" Tom asked.

"Not exactly," his father said thoughtfully. "Except that 'Dog' may bear some significance to where Ned's being held captive."

"Well, according to his message, Uncle Ned will be safe for eight days," Tom declared. "So we'd better find out what or where 'Dog' is and fast!"

Mrs. Newton and Phyl were overjoyed when notified of the missing man's message, and Tom assured them that he would start a search as soon as possible.

During dinner, the Swifts discussed nothing else but what method would be best in hunting for Ned Newton.

"I wish we could risk getting in touch with Uncle Ned," Tom said. "We could find him much quicker."

Remembering the explicit warning "Don't Contact," Mr. Swift advised:

"We'd better not jeopardize Ned's situation—those pirates might use desperate means of retaliation against him."

Father and son finally decided that, assuming he was somewhere on the Atlantic, using a submarine was the most feasible means of locating Uncle Ned.

After the meal, Tom and his father went to Mr. Swift's first-floor den which opened onto a terrace. Their conversation turned to the pirates and their victims.

"Dad," said Tom, "since the people on the ships have no warning before they're knocked out and show no physical injuries, it seems to me the pirates must be using a high-frequency sonic wave—one that affects nerve centers of the body."

"It sounds reasonable," Mr. Swift agreed. "If the passengers hadn't heard a plane each time, I might have suspected the use of a homing weapon. The kind that carries a beam projector—an unarmed torpedo which picks up the sound of the ship's screw and follows her to a certain point before releasing the beams. But your idea is a more logical one."

"Looks as if we'll have to turn detective to solve

this mystery," Tom remarked. "And speaking of mysteries, Dad, I picked up this strange coin today on the runway."

He handed the peso to Mr. Swift, who looked at it curiously. "This is certainly odd," he remarked.

Tom explained about finding it after Sidney Dansitt's plane had nearly run him down and repeated the science student's evasive reply when asked about the coin.

Mr. Swift stroked his chin thoughtfully. "You think Dansitt might have been lying?"

"From the way he reacted, yes."

The conversation turned to the jetmarine. Tom laid the coin on a table and then took from his pocket some new sketches he had made for the water intake ports on the submarine. Suddenly a whining sound, growing louder momentarily, broke the stillness inside the house.

"The burglar alarm!" Tom cried. "Somebody's trying to break in!"

This alarm went off whenever the magnetic field surrounding the Swift home became activated. To avoid its constant buzzing, the family wore deactivators in their wrist watches.

Tom and his father picked up two five-cell flashlights and rushed out the French doors of the den. Their powerful lights stabbed the darkness but picked up no one. By this time the Swifts' two bloodhounds were barking furiously in their kennels.

"Somebody's on the grounds all right," Tom said. "I'm going to let the dogs out."

He had barely reached the kennels when a scream shattered the stillness of the night! Tom whirled in his tracks.

"That cry—it came from the house!" he exclaimed worriedly.

CHAPTER 3

A BREAKNECK CHASE

WHO HAD screamed?

Tom raced toward the house. As he drew near it, his father joined him. Reaching some shrubbery at the side of the house, they stopped short. Sandy was standing there, speechless, staring at a figure which lay unconscious at her feet. Mrs. Swift rushed from the house as Tom played his flashlight on the unconscious form.

Bud Barclay!

Tom knelt to examine his friend. "He has a bad bruise over his right eye. Looks as though he was slugged."

In a couple of minutes his efforts to revive Bud were rewarded by a faint groan. The flier blinked, moaned, and struggled to stand. But a moment later he fell back.

"Take it easy, old man," Tom advised.

After one more attempt, Bud was able to sit up. He grinned weakly.

"I'll be all right as soon as my head clears a bit," he gasped. Then, suddenly recalling what had happened, he asked, "Did you catch him?"

"Who?" Tom asked quickly. "We didn't see anyone."

"Too bad," Bud said. "As I was coming along this side of the house I saw a man sneaking around from the back. I waited for him to get closer so I could tackle him."

"Is that when he hit you?" Sandy asked.

"No, not then. I decided to warn you Swifts. I tossed my penknife through the magnetic field, knowing it would touch off the alarm in the house and you'd come to see what was wrong. Then I began to trail him."

"Where to?" Tom asked.

"I shadowed him as he was sneaking toward the house. But he must have sensed I was behind him. Just as you rushed out and I was about to jump him, he whirled around and kayoed me. By the way, the man was masked."

"We owe you a million thanks, Bud," Mr. Swift said gratefully. "If you hadn't come on the scene, the intruder might have stolen some of our top-secret data."

The group went through the French doors into Mr. Swift's den. As Sandy was offering to get a cold compress for Bud's eye, Tom cried out:

"That Cuban coin! It's gone! So that's what the fellow was after!"

"And he helped himself to your sketch of the sub while he was here," Mr. Swift pointed out.

"It was too rough a sketch, fortunately, to be of much use to anyone," his son said.

"But how did that man get in?" Mrs. Swift asked. "There wasn't any second alarm."

Tom and his father looked at each other gravely. The intruder apparently knew how to keep the alarm from sounding!

"Our visitor was no small-time burglar but a scientist," Tom remarked.

Mr. Swift was thoughtful. "I can understand somebody wanting the sub sketches," he said. "But who'd want that coin? It must have some special significance."

"Do you know anybody who might want it, Tom?" Bud Barclay asked.

"Yes, I do," Tom replied. "Sidney Dansitt. He's the only outsider who knew I had the coin. What puzzles me is why he wanted it back so badly that he'd break in here to get it."

"It's a poser," Mr. Swift agreed. "The coin must have been what he was really after because he couldn't possibly have known you'd bring the sub plans to the house, Tom."

"Just the same I hate to have those drawings in such a person's hands," Tom replied. "I was stupid to leave them here in plain sight," he chided himself.

Sandy, quiet for the past minute, longed for action. "Why don't we let the bloodhounds out and see if they can pick up the thief's trail?"

"Good idea. He's probably still picking his way through the woods to the side road," Tom said.

Running quickly across the lawn, Tom and Sandy reached the kennels. The dogs set up a furious noise, welcoming their owners. Tom unfastened the gate, and after leashing them, led the bloodhounds to the terrace. They sniffed about for a couple of minutes without picking up the stranger's scent. Then suddenly they started off in excited pursuit, their noses to the ground.

Tom and Sandy were soon running at top speed to keep pace with the racing bloodhounds, who now pulled wildly at their leashes. In a short while brother and sister were plunging after the dogs into the dark woodland near their home. Tom beamed his powerful flashlight through the gloom as the hounds, alternately baying and sniffing, led him and Sandy in a zigzag route among trees and thickets.

"This is like trying to find a piece of a fractured atom," Sandy sighed.

"Guess you're right, Sis," Tom said, then exclaimed, "Listen! I hear someone!"

As the dogs increased their fearful yelps, Tom thrust his leash into Sandy's hand and dashed ahead. No doubt about it, the fugitive was only fifty yards ahead, crashing through the undergrowth. Foot by foot, Tom gained on the fleeing man.

"Stop!" the young inventor shouted.

The fugitive paid no attention to the command. As Tom narrowed the gap, he realized that the man probably had a car parked on the side road and hoped to make a getaway in it.

A minute later there was the roar of a motor. A

car hidden among the trees was starting up as Tom dashed out of the woods.

Tom hurled himself at the rear bumper. At the same moment the driver, applying frantic acceleration, spun the rear wheels. Dirt and leaves were flung into the young inventor's face. He missed the bumper by inches and lay panting on the ground as the car bounced onto the road and raced off.

"Tom, Tom, are you hurt?" Sandy cried, running up and bending over her brother.

"Nothing but a face full of mud," he replied ruefully. "The worst of it is, I didn't see the license plate of that sneak thief. Well, we may as well return the dogs to the kennel."

After locking them up, Tom and his sister walked slowly back to the house, discussing the eventful day. Uncle Ned's capture; Tom's and Sandy's narrow escapes; the run-in with Sidney Dansitt; the finding and losing of the dog's-head coin; the theft of the submarine sketches; and now the fleeing thief.

The next morning at breakfast Tom was still on the subject.

"I'm sure there's a tie-in between the place where Uncle Ned is and that stolen dog's-head coin," he told his father. "I'll bet the thief who was here last night is one of the pirates!"

"You mean if he were Dansitt, the student is a pirate?" Mr. Swift asked.

"Yes. Our dispatcher says he does a lot of flying—long trips at times," Tom answered. "He might even work the secret pulsator that we think causes the blackouts among the ship's passengers!"

"Hold on, Tom," his father warned. "That's a big job for a science student."

"I'll bet college is just a cover-up for Sidney Dansitt," Tom declared. "Dad, I wonder if the pirates' pulsator is like the one I'm experimenting on for the government."

"I hope not," the elder scientist said. "That's top secret."

"It gives me an idea, anyway," said Tom. "Not long ago I figured out a distorter that could neutralize my pulsator. If the distorter could be used against the pirates' plane, their blackout technique might be effectively stopped."

"A large order, Tom," his father said, but his own eyes showed as much excitement about the idea as his son's. "Where would you mount the distorter? On ships which the authorities might suspect would be attacked?"

"No, Dad. That would mean either building several distorters or always moving the one machine from ship to ship. I believe I'll put it on the jetmarine."

Tom went on to say that he could then act as a convoy for a freighter which might be a likely victim. When the invaders' plane swooped over the ship, he could stop its blackout ray by neutralizing the pulsator. As the pirates boarded the supposedly helpless freighter, they would be faced by armed men, probably Marines, not unconscious passengers and crew members.

"An excellent plan," Mr. Swift said enthusiastically.

Tom continued excitedly, "If the pirates did learn about the scheme and should escape, I could trail their ship or sub and maybe find out where Uncle Ned is."

"I can see that the pirates are all but captured." Mr. Swift grinned. "Well, good luck. And if I can help you, let me know, Tom."

"Thanks, Dad. But I'll try to get along alone. You're mighty busy yourself on that panfrequency thermopile for measuring solar radiation."

The older inventor nodded, then looked at his watch and remarked that there was just time to listen to the morning radio news before he and Tom started for work. He turned in his chair and switched on a set which was built into the corner cupboard back of him. The first bit of news electrified everyone in the family.

"We bring you a special bulletin," the broadcaster said. "The Coastways Steamship Line has just reported that one of its freighters, the *Neptune,* was raided a few hours ago. Money, jewelry, and a cargo of uranium were stolen. All passengers are safe. A representative of the McIntosh and Dansitt Steamship Company, owners of the *Neptune,* is unable to throw any light on the attack. And so another assault on American shipping occurs without explanation. And now a word from our sponsor—"

"Dad, do you think there could be any connection between Sidney Dansitt and the firm of McIntosh and Dansitt?" Tom asked, struck by the similarity of names.

"It's a possibility, of course," Mr. Swift replied. "But why would a pirate raid his own ship?"

"I don't know, except to throw the authorities off the trail," said Tom. "I think I'll check with the college dean about Sidney and his family. I might turn up with a real clue for finding Uncle Ned."

CHAPTER 4

SUBMARINE BLACKOUT

TOM DECIDED that his plan for finding out more about Sidney Dansitt would have to be postponed temporarily. He had an appointment with one of the engineers, Sid Baker, for nine that morning to test the maximum pressure which the hull of the jet-marine would stand. It was already eight fifteen.

"Ready to leave, Dad?" he asked.

When his father nodded, they said good-by to Mrs. Swift and Sandy and walked down the road. Half an hour later the two inventors reached Swift Enterprises and went their separate ways.

Tom hopped into his jeep, picked up Sid Baker, and drove across the grounds to the construction shed. Beaming his electronic key on the massive sliding door, he waited for it to open, then walked into the roar of milling machines, lathes, and riveters. The noise was intensified by irregular white flashes of light from the acetylene welding torches.

"They're welding the conning tower and snorkel

onto the sub right now," Baker shouted. "She won't be ready for the pressure test before noontime."

"In that case I may postpone the test a few hours," Tom remarked. "I want to rig up a distorter on the sub, as you would a snorkel, to see how it might work while the jetmarine's under water."

"Okay, Tom. Let us know when you're ready," Baker said.

The young inventor left then, asking to be notified the instant work was completed on the jetmarine. In the meantime, he would check up on Sidney Dansitt.

Returning to his jeep, he headed for the recently completed three-story laboratory building. Tom braked the car at the elevator shaft, flicked the lift combination, and drove aboard. Three floors up, at his lab level, he propelled the jeep onto the silent conveyor belt and whisked down the corridor of the quarter-mile-long plant wing. Using the automatic parker at the entrance to his private lab, Tom moved the jeep off the belt.

Going at once to the telephone, Tom put in a call to Grandyke University, where Dansitt was registered. He asked to speak with Dean Allsopp, whom he knew well.

"Hello, Tom," the man said cordially. "When are you and your dad coming out to lecture to our science classes again and tell what you're doing—or is it all top secret?"

"Most of it," Tom replied. "But thank you for the invitation. I was phoning to get a little information, Dean Allsopp. It's about a graduate student named

Sidney Dansitt." Tom gave the dean a quick résumé of his suspicions.

"Another complaint!" the dean exclaimed. "That's all I've heard about Dansitt lately. Confidentially, we're thinking of asking him to leave Grandyke."

"Would you mind telling me why?" Tom asked, interested at once.

"No, I don't mind," Dean Allsopp replied. "Dansitt's wild. Besides, he comes and goes as he pleases, taking trips away from here for three and four days at a time."

"Do you know where he goes?" Tom questioned. "That's one of the things I called about."

"No, I don't. But it's always in his plane, I understand."

Tom was disappointed that the dean did not know Dansitt's destinations. He asked for information about the student's family and was not surprised to learn that he was the son of the Dansitt who was a partner in the McIntosh and Dansitt shipping company.

"Sidney is very different from his hard-working, conscientious father and his charming mother," Dean Allsopp went on. "Spoiled son of a rich man is my guess. It's too bad. Sidney has an unusually good mind. He could be a most successful scientist if he would only settle down."

Tom asked several other questions, but the Dean could give him no information about the dog's-head coin or the names of the Coastways Line ships. The conversation ended with a promise on the dean's part to call Dansitt to his office and find out where he had been the night before.

"If I have anything worth while to report, I'll phone you, Tom," he assured him and hung up.

Without a ship registry handy, Tom decided to ask the Swifts' Central Seaboard telecaster for the data he wanted. A few moments later he was talking with Rick Dalton.

"Find out, will you, if any of the ships involved in these Caribbean attacks besides the *Neptune* belong to McIntosh and Dansitt," Tom requested.

"Let you know pronto," Dalton agreed.

Fifteen minutes later the videophone signal flashed red in the inventor's office.

"Boy, you sure get results fast." Tom laughed.

"I 'coptered over to the Port Director's office and got the info," Dalton said. "Just a five-minute hop across the harbor.

"The *Neptune* is the only ship which has been attacked that belongs to McIntosh and Dansitt."

"Good work, Rick!" Tom thanked him. "Signing off."

For several minutes after that Tom sat lost in thought. What was the best way to proceed with this new clue? At last he roused himself.

"I'm convinced Sidney Dansitt's mixed up in these strange raids, but actually I haven't any real evidence against him," Tom decided. "I'd better concentrate on improving the distorter and getting my sub in the water."

For three hours he worked on the gadget to reduce the vibration it showed when turned on. Tom watched the dials hopefully to see if the indicator flicker would cease. At last a broad smile spread over his face. He had succeeded! Even the faint hum that had been in the distorter carriage was gone completely.

Elated, Tom was about to switch off the instrument when he was startled by a booming voice. It came over the speaker's tube from the watchman's office at the main gate.

"Hey, Tom!" the unmistakable voice cried. "How about entertainin' an ole friend?"

Tom ran to the speaker and in an exaggerated drawl cried, "Chow Winkler, you ole Texas panhandler! You git right on up here! I sure didn't expect you back from Texas so soon."

Turning off the distorter, Tom went to the door of the laboratory to await the arrival of the former chuck-wagon cook who was now chef on all Swift expeditions. The roly-poly man appeared presently, straddling a company motor scooter.

Traveling thirty miles an hour down the conveyor belt, he looked like a happy cowpoke riding a small pony. In a matter of seconds Chow reached the laboratory and climbed awkwardly off his mount. As Tom strode out to greet him, the cook said:

"How come you talkin' Texas talk, Tom? You fixin' to pull up stakes an' relocate a little west of the Pecos?"

"No, pardner," Tom drawled. "Jest tryin' to make you feel at home, that's all!"

"An' what kind of an invention are you cookin' up now?"

Tom told him about the two-man atomic sub.

"Well, I'll be roped an' hawg-tied! Why, brand my periscope!" Words almost failed the amiable cook. "A lil' ole atomic baby sub, eh?"

Chow whistled in amazement, then became serious.

"Only one thing wrong, Tom," he continued a little sadly. "You ought to make this here critter a three-man job. Slap a galley onto 'er an' take ole Chowhead along with you!"

"Sure would like to have you with us," Tom agreed. "But you'd better stay ashore holding a line on us so we won't get lost."

The banter ceased when Tom told Chow about Ned Newton's capture. The Texan was all for going after the pirates at once.

"But right now, how about me rustlin' up a little lunch for you, Tom?" the cook suggested. "You rush around like a pup what's et loco weed, but you don't never think about food."

Tom laughed. "Okay. But don't give me whatever it was that made that waistline of yours stretch out." He looked critically at the cook's size fifty-two belt.

Chow grimaced and hurried off to the laboratory's kitchenette. While he was preparing a three-course dinner, Tom got in touch with Baker and also his two special friends in the plant, Arvid Hanson, the head of the model-making division, and Hank Sterling, chief patternmaker.

"We'll have the pressure test at four o'clock," he

told them and said he would like Hanson and Hank to be there. "By that time the distorter will be bolted onto the sub. I want to find out what may happen to it if it's subjected to great pressure."

The men promised to be on hand, saying that they would not miss the test for anything less than an air raid. According to Tom's calculations, they thought the small submarine should be able to descend easily to the unexplored depths of the ocean.

"We'll soon know," he said excitedly.

It was hard for the young inventor to keep his thoughts on the sumptuous meal Chow brought. He ate absent-mindedly, and when the cook pretended to be hurt, Tom laughingly said he was not sure how much pressure the butterflies in his stomach could stand.

"Butterflies?" Chow shouted. "You call these little golden-brown fish butterflies!" Then he grinned. "Oh, you mean you're fluttery inside. Brand my ten-gallon, that's the way I used to feel when a stampede was headin' for my chuck wagon."

In the end he ate most of Tom's lunch as well as his own. The inventor left him and phoned for mechanics to come and move the submarine to the tank where the pressure test would take place.

Twenty minutes later the jetmarine stood at the edge of the mammoth concrete tank which had been set in bedrock at one end of the Enterprises grounds. The sub's sleek black hull, with its transparent nose designed for greatest visibility, gleamed in the afternoon sunshine.

Tom directed the placing of the distorter on the top stern section of the submarine and helped to bolt it fast. Everything was now ready. The flat, cylindrical sonar transducer had already been mounted in a "bird cage" housing forward of the conning tower. A fathometer of similar design extended beneath the prow of the sub. There were a few last-minute adjustments, then the jetmarine was hoisted from its carriage into the giant tank and cradled securely.

At this moment Mr. Swift and Bud walked up. Tom smiled. "You're right on schedule," he said. "We're just about set for the pressure test."

Presently everyone was out of the sub and Hank called, "You can go in any time, Tom!"

"Good luck, son," Mr. Swift said as the young inventor jumped to the deck of the sub.

Water, shooting into the tank from four-inch nozzles, was flooding the compartment at the rate of two feet per minute.

Tom disappeared down the hatch, closing and securing the cover behind him. The engineers gave the bridge and distorter a final check, then stepped back. The two-foot-thick, steel double doors to cover the tank were swung upward by an overhead crane and bolted.

Tom Swift was now doubly sealed inside his newest project. In six more minutes the tank would be completely flooded. A hush fell over the watching group when the time was up.

Hank pulled gently on the pressure lever and the test began!

The butterflies in Tom's stomach were forgotten as he eagerly watched the indicators on the gauges creeping upward.

"It's working swell!" he murmured, elated.

Tom felt the hull shudder as the intense force increased. The jetmarine was now withstanding a pressure equal to that of a mile under the sea!

Suddenly Tom felt strange. His left side went limp, and he began to struggle for air. Realizing that he needed oxygen, Tom reached out with his right hand to open the valve of the emergency tank. Then he would push the signal button for the test to end.

Tom failed to reach either of them. His arm fell against his side and he keeled over!

CHAPTER 5

A PIRATE RAID

UNAWARE THAT TOM lay helpless inside the jetmarine, Mr. Swift and the rest of the group waited around the massive concrete pressurizer as the test period ended. There was no signal from Tom.

Presently Mr. Swift looked at his watch. "It's three minutes overtime," he said anxiously.

"Don't worry about Tom," Bud advised. "He's probably so engrossed in the tests that he has lost track of time."

Seconds ticked by. The engineers exchanged worried glances. Mr. Swift, too, looked apprehensive.

"Lower the pressure!" he called out anxiously.

Hank Sterling's hand flew to the valve and gave it a turn. The quiet hiss of escaping air was heard as the water's pressure against the hull lessened, pound by pound.

"Easy does it, Hank," Baker warned. "If you lower the outside pressure too fast, the sub's neutralizer may go out of commission or cause strains in the sub's hull."

Hank nodded in silent agreement. His eyes were glued to the pressure gauge. After the needle moved to zero, the water was quickly drained from the tank and its doors opened. Mr. Swift stared at the circular escape hatch of the submarine, expecting it to open. But the hatch remained closed.

The men waited for some sign from Tom. But seconds passed, then a minute without their hearing from him.

"Why doesn't he come out?" Bud muttered to himself.

Suddenly Mr. Swift sprang into action. "Bud," he called, "something *has* gone wrong! Bring that hydraulic jackscrew over here. We'll have to force the hatch open!"

With the men taking turns, the hatch was sprung. They pulled on the door in unison and finally it gave way. Bud leaped down the ladder. Inching his way forward he found Tom sprawled face down. Lifting the limp form across his back, he crawled amidships to the open hatch.

Mr. Swift and Hank reached down and relieved Bud of his burden. Gently they laid Tom on the submarine's deck and applied artificial respiration. When he did not respond, Mr. Swift said grimly:

"We'd better get him under an oxygen tent."

Tom was quickly carried to the first-aid station and placed under a tent. Within five minutes he began to regain consciousness.

Through the window of the oxygen tent, the anxious watchers could see Tom's chest rise and sink in an even, reassuring motion.

Twenty minutes later the lifesaving apparatus was opened. Tom's eyes flickered and he turned his head. Then, with an unexpectedly quick movement, he sat up, blinked, and looked around at the men.

"What happened? Who pulled the black shade down? Where the dickens am I?" he asked.

Mr. Swift's face broke into a smile of relief. "What a scare you gave us!" he said.

"You sure were out cold, inventor boy," Bud added.

Tom smiled wryly as the others explained about the accident and his rescue.

The engineers, meanwhile, had searched feverishly for the cause of the mishap. Hanson came up with the answer—a crimp in the copper tubing had cut off the oxygen supply.

"We'd better get you right home for some rest, son," Mr. Swift said. "You've had a mighty narrow escape."

At the others' insistence Tom spent the evening quietly, but after a good night's sleep he was ready for further tests on the jetmarine and the distorter. To his delight, he found that the distorter had withstood the assault of both the water and the pressure perfectly.

As Bud ambled into the laboratory and was about to ask when the periscopic camera would be installed on the submarine, the videophone signal flashed on.

"Might be another call from Rick Dalton," Tom remarked, walking over to the control board.

The sound came through before the picture cleared. A voice was saying excitedly:

"Hello! Hello! Tom! Come in!"

When the picture tumbled into place, it did not reveal Dalton. Instead, it was Ted Elheimer, the Swifts' Western telecaster.

"Hi, Ted!" Tom began. "What's all the excitement about?"

"I'm in New Mexico—in the desert!" was the tense reply. "Got a sensational story! Only two hours ago a whole construction crew of sixty men was knocked colder than a row of ice cubes! They were out for about twenty minutes. Everybody's wondering if there's any connection between this mysterious attack and the ones on those ships."

"It certainly sounds so," Tom replied. "Was the place robbed?"

"It sure was. I'll put a couple of the men on to tell you about the attack."

An alert-looking man in khaki work clothes stepped into view. "I'm an engineer on this job," he began. "Jerry Wilson's the name. We're working on a natural-gas pipe line. Our men were spread out over an area of about a square mile. It was nine o'clock your time when we blacked out. Last thing I remember I was watching some of the men join two sections of pipe."

"Didn't you feel anything at all?" Tom asked.

"Absolutely nothing," Wilson answered.

"Did you see or hear anything?" Tom went on.

"Let's see now. Yes, I vaguely remember hearing the noise of a jet plane just before I blacked out."

Elheimer introduced another man. He gesticulated wildly as he shouted:

"We've been robbed! I had the crew's pay for a month—nearly fifty thousand dollars—and it's gone! The money was flown in from Santa Fe not more than an hour ago."

"And no trace of it?" Tom asked.

"Not one. Every worker was unconscious, so it couldn't have been an inside job," the paymaster replied. "We've had plenty of robberies out here but this one's got us beat."

Elheimer interrupted to say that State Patrol officers were arriving by helicopter and he must sign off. He would let the Swifts know of any further developments.

"Well, mastermind," Bud said to Tom, "how are you going to figure this one out? It kind of knocks your theory about submarine pirates right up with the birdies."

Tom was both puzzled and worried. Here he was bending every effort to rescue Uncle Ned by submarine when the man might be in New Mexico! Of course the pirates could be using one or more amphibians in their work. Picking up the telephone, Tom called the nearest Air Patrol office. After introducing himself, he said:

"What's the situation around the Caribbean and other places in regard to amphibian planes? Any you know of in the hands of people who couldn't pass a security test?"

After a wait of ten minutes Tom received an answer. According to the records no amphibian craft had been reported being used in the Caribbean, or anywhere else, by persons whose character was not above reproach. Tom expressed his thanks and hung up.

"That washes out one hunch," he told Bud. The young inventor snapped his fingers. "You know, I believe the desert robbery was planted just to throw the authorities off the track."

"And fifty grand isn't to be overlooked, either, detective boy," Bud remarked, grinning, "especially with such an easy way to make the grab. I think the pilot with the pulsator landed and pulled off the robbery."

"Perhaps. But more likely he had an accomplice conveniently arriving by car after the whole camp was rendered unconscious," Tom replied. "It would be simple to scoop up a pay roll and get a good distance away in twenty minutes or so."

"Well, what's our next move?" Bud asked. "Does the team of Swift and Barclay go on a pirate hunt in the jetmarine or not?"

"It sure does. As soon as we get a clue to their hideout. How about your working on that while I install the periscopic camera and see about the water intake ports?"

"Okay. Operation Bowwow for me," Bud said and gave a few yelps.

Together the boys rode down the conveyor and drove to the construction shed. Tom was slightly annoyed to see the jetmarine still outside the shed. As he was about to order it wheeled inside—as a precaution against spying eyes—he and Bud heard the roar of a plane's motor overhead. They both glanced up quickly.

"Oh, oh! We're having company," Bud said, pointing.

The visiting plane was circling the Swift Enterprises boundaries.

"That's Dansitt's plane! What's he doing in our restricted area?" Tom exclaimed angrily.

The plane came in closer and lost altitude. It banked sharply, angling straight in toward the jetmarine. Suddenly a door swung open underneath the fuselage and a large black object appeared.

"A reconnaisance camera!" Bud shouted.

CHAPTER 6

A BOLO PUNCH

DANSITT'S PLANE, having completed its picture-taking run over the jetmarine, streaked westward at treetop level.

"Bud, I'm going after that guy and get those pictures back before he can develop them!" Tom cried angrily.

"You mean chase him? I don't think he'd dare land now that he knows you saw him taking shots of the sub."

"He'd dare anything," Tom replied bitterly.

With a roar Dansitt's plane came back and headed for the commercial field at the construction company plant.

"Drive me over while I get into my flying gear, will you?" Tom asked Bud.

"Sure thing."

The two boys leaped into the jeep and Bud drove at top speed to the field while Tom pulled on boots and put on the helmet he kept in the car.

"Even if Dansitt did get pictures of the sub," Bud remarked, "what good would they do him?"

"It's not the sub," Tom replied. "The distorter's in full view. That gives away my secret. If Dansitt is the pilot who works the blackout pulsator—"

"I get you, chief," Bud said. "It's a mean twist. But maybe you're giving Sidney credit for more brains than he has."

Reaching the field, Tom was told by the dispatcher that Dansitt had not landed nor asked for clearance.

"Then maybe he's not coming down. In that case I'm going to try to find him!" Tom declared. "Ask to have a small job ready for me, will you?" he requested, dashing down the tower steps.

In a few minutes one was rolled out. At this instant he saw Dansitt's plane winging past the hills northeast of the field. Tom quickly swung himself into the plane. Using the twin rocket assists, the excited pilot made a short run and streaked off after the other plane.

Within a minute he was flying abeam of it. As Dansitt sneered at him, Tom signaled the pilot to land. In reply, Dansitt shook his fist. Then, without warning, he threw his stick forward and went into a screeching dive. Flying level a few feet off the ground, he headed straight for a large red barn.

"You fool, you'll kill yourself!" Tom muttered.

Dansitt hopped the barn deftly and disappeared up a narrow valley. Tom hung on his tail. For a few minutes they followed a sparkling stream, then headed toward a low mountain. Nearing it, Dansitt zoomed up, skimming the treetops. Banking, he headed straight into the blazing sun. Tom clung fast in pursuit.

Suddenly Dansitt, maneuvering quickly, shot up into a tight loop and came in above Tom's tail, forcing him lower and lower. Tom countered with a sudden climb of his own and angled so that his enemy had to roll violently to the right. Tom banked sharply and went in on Dansitt's tail again.

In a desperate move to get away Dansitt dived his plane, almost cutting the grass in a wide meadow. A split-rail fence loomed ahead of him. Dansitt's right wing tip nicked it!

"I guess that scared him," Tom muttered as Dansitt cut his power, lowered his wheels and flaps, and went into a wide gradual turn toward an open field. He timed his approach expertly and touched the wheels on the ground just beyond a high wire fence.

Tom swung around and slipped his plane into the same field, rolling to a stop not more than twenty feet from Dansitt's ship. By this time Dansitt had climbed out and was running away from his plane.

"Stop!" Tom cried. "I want that film!"

Dansitt paid no attention to Tom. The young inventor darted after his enemy, and being more fleet-footed than Dansitt, soon overtook him.

Dansitt, however, wheeled about suddenly and lashed out viciously with his fists. But Tom nimbly dodged the intended blows and knocked the other to the ground with a cross-body block.

"Where's the film?" Tom cried as he pinned down his adversary's arms.

Instead of answering, Dansitt gave a sudden upward lurch, forcing Tom to loosen his grip. But before his opponent could slip completely from his grasp, Tom clamped Dansitt's arms again in a steellike grip. This time he straddled the other pilot. In doing so he felt a hard square object press against his thigh. Was it the film?

Tom tightened his grip on Dansitt

"Give me those pictures!" Tom demanded fiercely.

"Okay. Let me up and you can have them," Sidney Dansitt mumbled.

Tom bounded to his feet and waited. Dansitt took a box containing a roll of film from under his jacket and handed it over.

Tom took it but said he wanted to look inside Dansitt's camera. Without a word the photographer led the way back to the plane and opened the camera. There was no film inside.

"Satisfied?" he snapped.

"Okay," Tom conceded. "But you had no business flying over Swift Enterprises," he added hotly.

The other sneered. "The air's free and I was just having a little fun. But you got the film, so what are you griping about?"

"There's another matter I want to settle with you, Dansitt," Tom said. "How do you explain why some plans and the dog's-head coin disappeared from my home?"

Dansitt's eyes showed alarm for a fraction of a second, then they narrowed, gleaming cold and cruel, straight into Tom's.

"If you're accusing me of being a thief, I'll—" He stepped menacingly toward Tom.

"You were the only person who saw me pick up that coin from the runway," Tom said evenly.

"Suppose I was?" Dansitt flared. "I didn't steal it. And nobody can call me a thief!"

Unexpectedly he lunged at Tom and drove a smashing uppercut to his chin. The young inventor staggered backward, and for several seconds everything seemed to swirl before his eyes. Tom's vision cleared just in time to see Dansitt leap into his plane and take off.

Although furious that Dansitt had caught him off guard and made a getaway, Tom was relieved to find the roll of film still in his possession. After breathing deeply for a few moments, he fully regained his equilibrium and climbed into his plane. He easily maneuvered the craft out of the level meadow and was soon headed for the Swift commercial field.

"I wonder how many pictures Dansitt took," Tom mused.

As he opened the box alongside him to look, a small object fell out of it onto the floor of the cockpit. Tom looked down and whistled.

A dog's-head coin!

Tom snatched up the silver coin. Could this peso be the same one that was stolen from the Swift home? It certainly was identical, Tom concluded. He was convinced beyond all doubt now that the dog's head etched on the coin held important significance for Sidney Dansitt.

"And," Tom told himself, "that wild pilot's going to have another visit from me pronto so I can find out!"

Placing the Cuban peso in a zippered pocket, he radioed for clearance. He set the plane down and taxied to a hangar. Bud Barclay was waiting for him.

"Wow! What a game of air tag!" he exclaimed. "Did you get the film or just a wallop on the jaw?" Bud eyed Tom's swollen chin curiously.

Holding up the box of film, Tom told the story of the chase and its rewarding climax.

"Now we'll go get some lunch."

"I'll believe that when the food's in front of me," Bud said. "How about me driving?"

"Go ahead," Tom said as they climbed into the jeep. "And now for something that will jar you loose from your moorings," he added, as Bud drove from the field onto the highway.

The inventor reached in his pocket and pulled out the dog's-head coin. Bud glanced at it and almost swerved off the roadway.

"How'd you get that again? Dansitt give it to you?" he asked.

"I don't think he knows I have it," Tom answered. "It was in with the film."

As Tom gazed at the dog's head, he noticed for the first time that there was a tiny hole in the peso. Wondering if it had been put there on purpose, he flipped the coin in his hand. On the obverse side was etched a full-length map of Cuba. Squinting at the pinhole, Tom studied its position in relation to the two sides of the coin.

"What are you doing?" Bud asked. "You look like a man gone money mad."

"Bud," said Tom excitedly, without taking his eyes off the tiny hole, "pull to the side of the road, will you? I want you to take a look at this!"

Bud parked the jeep and took the coin.

"Look where this hole comes through!" Tom said.

Holding the peso to the light, Bud closed his left eye and peered at the dog's head. "The hole's right in the middle of the collar," he said.

"Right. Now turn it over."

Bud obeyed, then remarked, "The hole appears to be off the north coast of Cuba."

"See any connection?" Tom asked.

"Not particularly," his friend replied, "except that the hole might indicate an island off the coast of Cuba or a spot in the ocean."

"And if such an island were shaped like a dog's head, we'd have a second clue," Tom added eagerly. "We'd probably find Uncle Ned there!"

"Good night!" Bud shouted.

"If Dansitt's one of the pirates," Tom said, "I can see why he'd want that coin back. The dog's head is probably the pirates' insigne."

"Say, who knows about the islands in that area?" Bud asked.

"Kane has spent a lot of time around Guantanamo Bay," Tom answered. "Knows that whole area. I'll call him."

"After we've had some grub, please," Bud begged.

When they reached the kitchenette in the laboratory, Chow Winkler took one look at Tom and cried, "Brand my lariat, you sure ran into a tough critter. Who was he?"

"A pirate with a bolo punch."

"You jest don't know how to stay out o' trouble, do you?" The cook wagged his head.

He prepared a hearty lunch for the boys, telling Tom a good square meal was the best way to restore one's fighting strength.

"But what do you do when it hurts to move your jaw?" Tom countered.

"You hand your plate over to me," Bud spoke up with a grin. "Three squares a day is hardly enough to keep me up to fighting strength."

After lunch Tom went to the videophone in his

laboratory and got in touch with Kane. After the young inventor had asked several questions, the telecaster said:

"I never heard of a place named Dog Island. About the closest thing to it is Cat Island." He chuckled. "But that's not in the region you're referring to."

Tom, bitterly disappointed by this information, was about to switch off the set when Kane almost shouted into the mike:

"I just remembered! There's a narrow channel running through the middle of a small island north of Porto Madre, actually making two islands. The channel is called the Dog's Collar!"

CHAPTER 7

IN ENEMY TERRITORY

TOM WATCHED the videophone screen intently as Kane sketched from memory a charcoal diagram of the island with the channel called Dog's Collar.

"One of the islands looks like the head of a springer spaniel!" Tom cried. "And the other like its shoulders. I can see how the channel got its name."

"I don't recall the name of the islands," the telecaster said. "But it's a doggy word, and I know I can get it for you. I'll call you back."

"Pin point it on the map for me, too, if you will," Tom suggested before he switched off the set.

"So Kane did my job for me, eh?" the copilot said. "It's a swell clue. At last we've found out what Uncle Ned meant by 'Dog.'"

"Yes. And when Kane obtains the rest of the info, we'll know exactly where Uncle Ned's prison is!" Tom added excitedly.

"Would you take a chance on getting through to him then?" Bud inquired.

Tom did not reply for a moment, as if weighing the advisability of such a move. Finally he shook his head.

"No. If the pirates intercepted any message to Uncle Ned, they might remove him to another hideout. Or do something even worse," Tom said soberly. "Anyhow, a lot of precious time would be wasted."

"You're right, owl boy. No sense tipping off that gang now," Bud remarked. "They have enough of a head start as it is."

"We'd better develop this film," Tom reminded his friend.

The two boys went to the developing room adjoining Tom's laboratory to find out how successful Dansitt had been. A few minutes later Tom cried:

"They're blanks!" The young inventor groaned. "I'll bet Dansitt kept the real shots and palmed this blank roll of film off on me!"

As Tom's brain swam with anger and self-reproach for letting himself be tricked, the telephone in the lab buzzed. Tom went to answer it. Fletcher, the dispatcher at the Swift Construction Company airfield, was on the wire.

"Hello, Tom!" his excited voice began. "I just overheard something you should know!"

"What is it?" Tom urged.

"It's about Sidney Dansitt," Fletcher said. "He returned here a little while ago. I was off duty and thought I'd watch him. The first thing he did was go to a phone and call a New York number. The name he mentioned sounded like 'Chilcote,' but I'm not sure. Dansitt said, 'I've got the shots of the Swifts' new sub.' "

Tom gasped. "Go on!" he urged.

"Then he told the fellow that he would leave immediately for New York with them. He took off about five minutes ago. I'd sure like to see you beat him to the punch. He's one guy I can't stand!" Fletcher concluded.

Tom told him about the blank roll of film and added, "Which field did Dansitt give as his destination?"

"Base Three for private planes," the dispatcher answered.

"Okay. Thanks a lot."

Tom hung up and told Bud of the latest development. "Chilcote may be one of the pirates," he added excitedly. "I'm going to try beating Dansitt to New York in the fastest jet we have. You stand by here for word from Kane, will you?"

"I'll eat and sleep in this spot," Bud agreed, and added that he would notify Tom's family of his departure.

As Tom quickly put on his leather flying jacket he asked Bud to telephone the field to have a plane warmed up for him.

"Okay," the copilot replied as Tom dashed from the laboratory.

By the time he reached the field, the jet was ready

for flight. Positive that he could overtake Dansitt, Tom soon had the craft in a vertical climb. When he gained enough altitude, he leveled off and headed for Manhattan.

By the time Tom reached the huge New York airport, darkness had fallen and the airstrip lights were blazing below. He brought the jet into the traffic pattern and landed.

"Get my plane out of sight as soon as possible," Tom instructed the mechanics.

The plane was rolled into a nearby hangar. Tom took a station near the flight-control desk, where he could keep an eye out for his enemy's arrival. Twelve minutes later he heard Dansitt's voice calling the tower for clearance to land. Tom dashed to the entrance of the building, hired a taxi, and asked the driver to stand by until he came out again. Then he went back to wait for Dansitt.

A few minutes later he saw Dansitt approaching one of the gates at a trot. In his right hand he was carrying a flat square package just like the one he had handed Tom.

Though he was sure that the package contained the film, Tom restrained an impulse to jump Dansitt and snatch the parcel from him. It would be wiser, he decided, to wait and possibly get a look at the person for whom the film was intended. And, Tom reasoned, only a scientist would be interested in having it, so whoever received the package from Dansitt's hands might be a lead to the mastermind of the pirates!

Keeping out of sight, Tom let his enemy walk past.

As Dansitt got into a taxi, Tom jumped into his and told the driver to follow the other car.

"Don't let it get away, driver!" he called from the rear seat.

"Say, what are you, a detective?" the taxi driver asked. "Where's your badge?"

Tom was stumped. Was the man going to refuse to co-operate? Instead of answering the question, he said:

"You've been reading about these Caribbean attacks, haven't you? Well, I think that guy ahead of us is one of the pirates!"

"Good night!" the man exclaimed. "That's enough for me. Here we go!"

In the wide stream of traffic that rolled toward the city, it was easy to remain close and still be unobserved by the cab driver and the passenger ahead. Along the parkways and into the center of the city itself, Tom's driver never let more than two or three cars get between his own cab and the one he was tailing.

On a crosstown street in the fashionable section of the East River, Dansitt hopped out of his taxi in front of a modern apartment house. Tom instructed his driver to park halfway down the block and wait for him. Then he slipped quietly out of the cab and made his way toward the wall of the house. From the sidewalk to about a foot over Tom's head the building was of black polished marble, which, together with the dim street lighting, afforded Tom a small dark pocket in which to conceal himself.

Dansitt, meanwhile, had shifted the package to his

left hand and was paying his driver. He obviously had given him a large bill, because the driver fumed and fumbled trying to make change. Finally Dansitt stepped to the bright entrance of the apartment house and looked at his watch. Turning about, he peered up and down the street.

Tom hugged the wall.

At that moment another taxi pulled up in front of the entrance. As Dansitt moved toward it, the passenger opened the door and stepped out.

Tom, after one look at the stranger, was sure he could never forget the man's face, with its long features and cruel but intelligent expression. Could this be the scientist?

Tom leaped away from the wall.

"Hold on, Dansitt. I want that film."

The student's jaw dropped in amazement when he recognized Tom, but quickly regaining his composure, he sneered, "It happens to belong to me, wise guy."

"For a scientist, you don't operate with the ethics of our profession," Tom accused him. "You sneaked those photos."

Dansitt glanced at his companion, standing beside him with fists clenched, and laughed sarcastically. "Ethics, bah! You're still wet behind the snorkel, boy!" Then he assumed a pose of bravado. Holding the package toward Tom, he rasped, "Okay, whiz kid. They're yours if you can get 'em!"

In one whirlwind motion Tom accepted the challenge. His arm flew out so fast that it was a blur in the darkness. He snatched the film, at the same time hurling his body against the two men. They fell to the sidewalk, the wind knocked out of them.

Thrusting the package under his jacket, Tom tugged the zipper upward and ran toward his waiting taxi.

Out of the corner of his eye he saw a burly doorman spring from the entrance toward him. Tom pivoted and plunged between two parked cars in an effort to get up the street to his taxi. His right leg caught against a rear bumper and he fell sprawling into the street.

As he started to get up, Tom saw the big doorman coming through the narrow space straight at him. At the same moment that the man flung himself forward, Tom shot his legs upward. The movement caught his assailant in mid-air with a stomach blow that sent him flying backward.

Tom scrambled to his feet, dashed to his cab, and climbed in. "Let's go!" he said.

The taxi roared ahead. Looking out the rear window, Tom saw the confused figures of Dansitt and his cohorts in the middle of the street. He pressed his hand to his jacket. The package was still there.

"Keep going crosstown for a few blocks!" Tom ordered the driver. "And then circle around to Grand Central Station."

Upon reaching the station, the taxi drew up to the curb. Tom thanked the driver, paid him from bills in his pocket, and added a generous tip.

The driver grinned and handed Tom a card with

his name on it. "Any time you want to chase a pirate again, give me a call."

"I'll do that, Mike."

Tom got out, mingled with the rushing crowd in the station, then walked to a hotel where he planned to spend the night. He had dinner, then hurried to a large photographic shop which remained open late.

"Can I have a film developed right away?" he asked a clerk.

"Afraid not," the man replied. "All the technicians have gone home."

"I could do it myself," Tom said eagerly. "All right if I use a darkroom?"

"Just so long as you identify yourself."

Tom reached in his hip pocket for his wallet with several identifying cards. It was not there!

"I— My wallet's gone!" he cried.

"Sorry," the man said, "but unless you—"

Remembering a letter he had with him, Tom produced it and showed the name and address to the clerk whose eyes opened wide.

"Tom Swift, eh? Well, help yourself to a darkroom. And if your wallet's been stolen, I'll lend you some money."

Tom thanked him, saying he had money in another pocket. On the way to the darkroom he decided that the wallet probably had dropped out during his scuffle with the doorman.

"I'll go back there as soon as I finish here and hunt for it," he told himself.

Tom inserted the film in a round tank, poured in

he developer, and timed it carefully. At the proper moment he took it out, washed, and hardened it. Then he held the film to the electric light.

"The sub! The distorter!" he muttered excitedly. "These are wonderful shots! Am I glad I got them away from Dansitt!"

After cleaning up the room, Tom hurried out, paid the clerk, and returned to the hotel. He arranged to have the negatives placed in the hotel's safe, then took a subway to the part of town where he had lost his wallet. He searched the sidewalk and street, but it was not in sight.

Another doorman was on duty. Following a sudden hunch, Tom decided to call upon the suspected scientist. But upon inquiry he was told that no one by the names of Chilcote or Dansitt lived there.

Disappointed, Tom went back to the hotel. Before going to bed he telephoned home. Mr. Swift answered. Tom told him about retrieving the film, then asked:

"Any word about that place with the dog collar?"

"No. But some other interesting news came in. Dalton called from Florida to say that Sidney Dansitt has been seen several times with a lawyer who works for McIntosh and Dansitt. His name's George Jennig. He might be involved in the piracies. Well, we'll see you in the morning."

"Sure thing, Dad."

After a restful night's sleep Tom took a taxi to the airport. Entering the hangar where his plane had been rolled, he saw that it was nowhere in sight.

"My name's Tom Swift. Where's my ship?" he called to a man who seemed to be in charge.

The other man stared at him in astonishment, saying, "You're Tom Swift?"

"Of course I am," Tom said, both puzzled and impatient at his reaction. "And I need my plane in a hurry!"

"Well," the man replied, "if you're who you say— it's tough luck. Your plane's gone."

"What!" Tom almost shouted. "What do you mean—*gone!*"

"All I know is, a man came here for the plane last night—he had all the proper credentials—and said he was Tom Swift."

CHAPTER 8

A WANTED SPY

"SOMEONE WAS posing as me!" Tom cried incredulously.

The hangar official nodded and said that the man who had taken Tom's plane had displayed a wallet with several cards.

"What did he look like?" the young inventor asked.

The description fitted Dansitt's friend at the apartment house! Tom groaned. There was no telling what the man might do with the credentials or the plane.

"Have you any idea where he was going?" the young inventor asked.

"Not exactly. But he did ask for a report on weather conditions south of here. They're not good. This is the hurricane season."

As Tom dashed to a phone, he wondered if his stolen plane was now at "Dog." He called the police and the Air Patrol, reported the theft, and gave a complete description of the plane and the suspect. Then he put in a call to Bud Barclay in Shopton. Tom told him what had happened and asked his friend to come for him.

"Use the *Sky Queen*," Tom advised. "And fly her wide open! I've got to find that guy who's using my name!"

"I'll start at once, skipper," Bud promised.

His call completed, Tom started checking on Dansitt and learned that he had left the airport at midnight in his own plane. He had not named his destination. Tom surmised that the student might have followed the man who had stolen the Swift plane.

"Say, Mr. Swift," the hangar official said suddenly, "I just remembered that the fellow who's got your plane left a raincoat here. Maybe there's something in the pockets."

He put in a call to the lost-and-found department and the coat was brought over. To Tom's disappointment, there was no identification as to its owner, but there were two rumpled mimeographed sheets.

Tom began to read the first page and was amazed to find it was a treatise on the military use of supersonic sound waves as an offensive weapon.

"The pirates' blackout method!" Tom murmured, his feeling of excitement mounting.

Tom's heart beat faster and more excitedly as he read. Flipping to the second page his eyes were attracted to the name of the writer at the bottom of the sheet. It was a name that Tom stared at, fascinated, for almost a minute—*Herman Chilcote*.

Tom's exultation hit a new high. Clues were coming thick and fast now.

"It shouldn't be hard to find Chilcote," he decided. "I'll ask Dad about him."

In a few minutes Tom was talking to his father on the phone and receiving an even greater surprise. Mr. Swift recalled the name at once and read his son a note from a scientific periodical.

> *"This Journal regrets to announce to its readers that Herman Chilcote has recently disappeared from his top-secret post with the British Government and is now being hunted by the authorities as a possible spy."*

"For Pete's sake!" Tom cried. "We're really up against a dangerous enemy."

"I'm afraid we are," Mr. Swift agreed. "I can't urge you too strongly, Tom, to watch your step where that renegade scientist is concerned."

After Tom finished talking with his father, he reread Chilcote's article slowly. The invention, he found, was not unlike his own.

"My distorter can certainly keep that fellow's blackout rays from working!" he thought elatedly.

Half an hour later Bud roared in with the *Sky Queen*. Tom climbed aboard and they took off at once.

"I set ten records getting here!" Bud laughed. "Bet I'll be back in Shopton in ten minutes!"

"Have a heart!" Tom cried. "I don't want us to blow up!"

On the way home Tom showed Bud the article by

Chilcote and told him about the man being wanted as a spy.

"He's probably the leader of the pirates," Bud surmised. "Well, when do the fireworks start? Do you figure he's holed up at 'Dog'?"

Tom shrugged. "The next move is a reconnaissance trip over the area to see what we can learn as soon as I hear from Kane."

"Why didn't you say so before?" Bud complained, banking the *Sky Queen* so he could head south.

"Oh, not in this ship," Tom said quickly. "The Flying Lab is too obvious. We'll take the photography job."

The boys reached Shopton in time to have lunch with the Swift family and told them about the plan for the reconnaissance flight. Before picking up the film needed for their photographic work, Tom checked on the jetmarine's progress. Installation of the radio equipment had just been completed and was being tested. Tom waited long enough to learn that it met his specifications, then went to his laboratory for binoculars.

He noticed the videophone's signal flashing and hurried over to turn on the instrument. The light stopped flashing and Kane appeared on the screen. He was standing in front of a detailed ocean chart.

"I found what you want, Tom," he began. "The place is called Spaniel Island. It's north of Porto Madre. 79 degrees west, 23 degrees north latitude. It's near the Santa Maria Keys in the Old Bahama Channel."

He pointed on the map with a pencil to the exact location.

"Thanks a lot," Tom said. "I may be seeing you."

As he switched off the set, Bud rushed in. "Say, skipper, I've just been checking the weather. It's not good in the Caribbean."

"I know. But we'll try to beat out any bad storms," Tom declared, and told Bud of Kane's report about "Dog."

"So Spaniel Island's the name of the pirates' hideout!" Bud exclaimed. "Let's go then! The photography plane is warmed up and ready to take off."

Bud enjoyed flying this interesting craft. It was essentially a large oval wing, with a full fuselage that gave plenty of room for the cameras. The plane, powered by two engines, had an extraordinary wing slot design that enabled it to glide along at fifteen miles an hour, excellent for photography purposes. But when speed was essential, the craft could race along at six hundred.

The boys walked to the airfield. While Tom was adjusting the binocular camera, Bud telephoned the weather bureau at Miami.

"How's the hurricane business these days?" he asked.

"A storm's brewing near Cuba," the observer replied. "But it shouldn't gain any real velocity for another twelve hours. We're going to send out small-craft warning signals in a few hours."

Bud gave Tom the weather observer's report. "We'd better make this a snappy trip," he advised.

Tom grinned. "Twelve hours? We'll be home and sound asleep before that hurricane gets too bothersome."

He gunned the starboard engine. The portside work horse roared to life and the cabin quivered in the powerful windstream. The ship taxied down the strip, swung about, and with a loud roar began her take-off.

They had been flying for half an hour when Bud remarked, "We've certainly passed a lot of government planes—seems as if they're all over the sky today."

"I suppose they're watching the shipping lanes carefully for more attacks," Tom remarked.

"You're convinced the pirates haven't moved their scene of operations despite that desert robbery, aren't you?" Bud asked.

"That's right. They may be doing some profitable long-distance work too, but I still think their base is here," Tom answered. "By the way, I forgot to tell you about the note I found on my desk from Dean Allsopp. Dansitt never went back to Grandyke after the night the coin was stolen from our house."

As the boys neared the Bahamas, the first angry gusts of wind whipped against the cabin.

"Looks as if the weatherman might have been wrong," Bud remarked. "That hurricane is no twelve hours away."

"I think you're right, Bud. We'll be bucking some pretty strong head winds in a few minutes."

Tom swept down over Andros Island and the boys

caught a glimpse of the brilliantly colored coral reefs.

"How many shots of Spaniel Island are you going to try for?" Bud asked.

"Two shots as we approach the island," Tom replied. "And one of Dog's Collar Channel when we pass over it. Of course the movie camera will be working the whole time."

"Is the place inhabited?"

"According to Kane it isn't," Tom replied. "Maybe a few fishermen."

As the plane gained altitude, the boys could see orderly rows of whitecaps forming below them. The sea was becoming choppy.

Tom adjusted a queer-looking gadget that he had clamped to the control panel.

"What on earth is that?" Bud asked.

"A portable sound-wave distorter," Tom replied. "Same principle as the big one I built for the jet-marine. I want to be sure that the pirates can't make us black out."

"Do you think they'd do that without the motive of robbery?" Bud asked.

"If they suspect who we are, yes. And especially if they find out we're taking pictures."

A haze began to form. It came in wisps, then in larger stretches.

"Our infrared film and red filter can cut through this stuff," Tom said. "I'd better check the cameras and make sure everything is in order. Take over, will you, Bud?"

"There's Santa Maria," Bud called. The island lay off in the distance, a bit to port.

"If you line up that high point with the last reef we'll have a perfect bead on Spaniel Island," Tom said.

Before they started to climb, the boys could see the wide-leafed palms being flattened almost to the ground by the rising wind. The plane shuddered with great violence from time to time.

"We're almost there!" Bud cried.

Tom took his position at the self-developing camera. "I wish we could go in slowly," he said, "but we'd better not risk it. We'll keep going right on past the islands while the pictures are developing. If we don't get what we want, we'll turn back and take more shots."

"Spaniel Island!" Bud shouted. The unmistakable head and shoulders of a dog were there, as clear as they had looked on the charts.

Tom glanced below. Somewhere on the islands beneath them was Ned Newton! Again he had to check a strong impulse to contact his uncle.

But the next instant, as Bud made his pass, Tom's hand flicked and he got the first two shots. A moment later he had one of the channel.

Without changing course, the plane labored straight on into the high winds. Tom unloaded the camera and studied the twin shots.

"There's not a thing unusual even in the channel." He groaned. "I'll have to take more pictures. Bring her about, Bud!"

The copilot followed instructions. He also picked up the powerful binoculars they had brought and studied the land. Suddenly he yelled:

"Tom, Spaniel Island has an airstrip, sure as shooting! On the dog's shoulders. What say we land?"

The inventor considered the startling idea as he took more pictures. He was just about to say they would risk it when a terrific gust of wind hit the plane and swung it around.

"The hurricane!" Bud cried.

The next instant the ship vibrated as if it would be torn apart, then dropped with sickening speed.

CHAPTER 9

ESCAPE SUITS

WITH THE PLANE dropping at the rate of two thousand feet a minute, Tom and Bud were at the mercy of the hurricane. Then suddenly they were buffeted upward at the same tremendous rate of speed.

As Bud worked frantically to pull the bouncing ship out of the vertical currents, it went into a whirlwind spin. The copilot's head banged hard against the window, stunning him.

Tom sprang forward and took the controls. He managed to throttle back, reducing speed, then increased the prop pitch. Most Caribbean hurricanes, Tom knew, travel northwest, and he decided to take a chance on a northeast direction.

Just then Bud groaned and rubbed the fast-swelling bump on his forehead. "Looks bad," he murmured.

"We'll pull out of it somehow," Tom replied tersely.

He peered intently through the swirling black cloud mass in which the plane was yawing and pitching. Suddenly he caught his breath. For a second he had glimpsed a tiny patch of white ahead. Hardly daring to hope, Tom steered straight for it. A few minutes later the plane was flying in clearing skies.

"You did it!" Bud exclaimed. He reached up and slapped his friend's shoulder. "I was a big help, conking out," he said glumly, "but next time I'll keep my wits about me."

"Can I count on that?" Tom grinned.

"By the way, windjammer boy," Bud asked, "where are we?"

"We were blown a good distance off course," Tom replied. "But now we're heading straight for Shopton. If you'll take over, I'll see if our movie camera brought any better results than the stills."

The copilot was in sight of land before Tom was able to report the result, but he was elated.

"They're good, Bud. You were right about an airstrip. In one corner of the dog's shoulder is a clump of trees that could be a camouflaged hangar."

"And I'll bet your stolen plane's sitting in there waiting to go out on another raid," Bud said in disgust.

Tom looked at his copilot in amazement. "Bud, you've hit on an idea! Those pirates could carry out their raids, using my plane to black out ships, and no one would suspect them."

As if to confirm the inventor's opinion, when Tom clicked on his home-beamed radio his father's voice came through clearly and excitedly:

"There's been another attack. Same pattern. This one was in Westbrook, a small town near Lake Erie. Every citizen within blocks of the center was knocked unconscious for nearly half an hour."

"Any robbery?" Tom asked.

"The local bank was cleaned out. A big haul," Mr. Swift answered. "Listen, Tom. Plane spotters on a nearby hill have reported every ship that passed over. Yours was one of them!"

Tom's eyes blazed. He determined that nothing would stop him from capturing the bandit who was flying it.

"When will you be back, Tom?" his father asked.

"Pronto."

Upon reaching his father's office in Shopton, Tom was disturbed by further news. He learned that the government had called off its watch on the Caribbean. Admiral Hopkins had notified Mr. Swift that all but one plane and one small fast destroyer had been removed from the area.

"I'm afraid that leaves things wide open for Dansitt, Chilcote, and the others," Tom said worriedly. "Dad, I think they're still around Spaniel Island. I'm going to get the jetmarine into the ocean right away and rescue Uncle Ned, even if I never do anything else!"

"Hold on, son! I promised your mother you wouldn't take off until you had perfected your escape suit. How about it?"

Tom smiled. "I've been working on that as a secret project. Bud has dubbed the suit the Fat Man."

Tom briefly outlined the principal features of the metal Fat Man. The body of it was egg-shaped and was five feet in diameter at the center. Inside an operator's seat had been built, surrounded by a number of instruments. There was also a quartz vision plate. This window would serve as entrance to the Fat Man.

Tom pointed out that the suit was propelled by air pressure and was equipped with small ballast tanks which would enable it to be manipulated like a tiny submarine. Two such Fat Men were to be installed in the jetmarine next to the decompression chamber, which had been designed to be opened either from the inside or the outside.

Mr. Swift listened intently as Tom continued, "But my main innovation, Dad, consists of the Fat Man's pantograph arms and legs. Hands and feet, too. I work them on button controls from inside. They're almost human."

The elder inventor raised his eyebrows. "How do you keep this gimmick from falling over?"

"Gyroscope!" Tom replied. "An automatic balancing brain."

"I'm convinced," Mr. Swift conceded. "But has it been tested with anyone inside?"

"No."

His father frowned. "It's one thing to test an invention in the abstract and another to imitate an actual experience."

"I'll do it late tomorrow morning, Dad. Tonight I'll check it."

"Excuse me, folks," said a deep voice from the open doorway, and Chow walked in. "I jest come to tell you my chuck wagon's outside, itchin' to feed you all." The cook grinned. "If you won't come an' get your victuals, well, brand my charcoal stove, I'm forced to fetch it to you."

He wheeled in a cart with several covered metal dishes kept warm over a flame and began to serve from them.

"I'd hate to starve, of course," Tom said with a grin, "but I'd rather do that than be—eh, poisoned. What's that funny colored stuff in the bowls?"

"Soup an' it's not—"

"Purple soup!" Tom exclaimed. "What did you put in it, iodine?"

Chow looked hurt. Then he appealed to Mr. Swift. "You know what it is, sir?"

"I'm afraid I don't," the older inventor replied.

"Well, brand my ole bean patch!" the cook said in amazement. "You jest taste that special o' mine. It's snappin' turtle right from the Rio Grande stewed up with red cabbage."

"Ugh! What a fate for a poor turtle!" Tom groaned.

Chow made no reply to this, and after a dark look from the Texan, Tom put his spoon into the concoction and tasted it.

"I can't tell where the turtle stops snapping and the cabbage leaves," he said, "but this is pretty good after all."

The cook grinned in relief but waited to watch father and son finish their portions. As he served the rest of the meal, Mr. Swift said:

"Tom, I must go to Florida on business. I've put it off as long as I can. Do you recall my friend Mr. Foster down there?"

"The one with the yacht? I'll never forget our cruise on the *Primrose* when I was a little boy and the fight with the shark," Tom replied.

His father's eyes lighted up too at the recollection. "Mr. Foster," he said, "wants to talk over an idea he has for an invention. He has suggested doing it on board ship. I've accepted on the proviso that we head for Spaniel Island."

"You may find Uncle Ned before I do," Tom remarked. "Let's make it a race." He laughed. "You have a head start, I have a faster craft." Then he sobered. "But what about those blackout attacks? Maybe you ought to take one of the distorters with you."

"Yes, I'll have one put aboard," his father said. "Although I doubt that the pirates will bother a yacht. They're after cargo of greater value."

"Very likely," Tom responded. "But that gang has proved to be a deadly enemy, and you're planning to head where the danger from them is greatest."

The older inventor laid a hand on his son's shoulder. "That's why I've decided to leave here secretly tonight and travel incognito. But as for the danger, you and I are in this together, Tom, to save a life."

The two exchanged understanding smiles and the

conversation turned to other topics. It finally reverted to the subject of the Fat Man, and Mr. Swift exacted a promise from Tom that the escape suit would be completely foolproof before he would start his trip.

At eleven o'clock the next morning, the time set for the test, a group gathered at the outdoor tank to watch the exhibition. With the engineers were Mrs. Swift, Sandy, and her friend Phyllis.

"Where are the actors?" Baker spoke up. "This is Tom and Bud's cue."

The two youths were in Tom's lab where the inventor was fusing two wires. Although he used no soldering iron or blowtorch, a weld was being produced!

Chow was looking on with something akin to fear in his eyes. "That jest ain't natural, Tom," he said. "Brand my coyotes, goin' against what's right."

Tom grinned. "What's the matter with coaxing a little fire from the sun to do your work? That pane of glass, Chow"—he pointed—"is specially ray absorbent."

"You mean it's jest a ole-fashioned burning glass?" the cook asked.

Tom nodded. "Only stronger."

The telephone rang and Chow answered. A peculiar look came over his face as he glanced at Tom. All he said was "Okay" and mysteriously left the room.

CHAPTER 10

A CRUCIAL TEST

BEFORE TOM AND BUD could leave the lab for the pressure test of the Fat Man, the call signal of the videophone flashed on. The boys stood still as the inventor tuned it in. Kane was revealed as Tom acknowledged that he was ready for the message.

"Big news!" the telecaster said. "A plane has just reported seeing a ship sink in the Caribbean. The odd thing about it is that there was no call for help—at least no one picked it up."

"The people on board might have been blacked out," Tom suggested. "What about survivors? Did they give the usual account?"

"Tom, there weren't any survivors," Kane replied. "It was a small freighter called the *Spray Cloud*. It's a pretty grim story."

"I'll say. The question is, did the pirates sink it or was there an accident aboard?"

"Sorry. I can't help you on that one," Kane said, adding, "Roger."

Tom clicked off the set and turned to Bud. "If we could find out what the cargo on the *Spray Cloud* was, I believe it might answer a lot of questions."

"Those poor guys," Bud murmured.

Tom had already picked up the phone and was asking a secretary to find out what shipping company owned the *Spray Cloud*. In less than a minute she replied:

"The North-South Atlantic Company, offices in New York City."

"Connect me with the traffic manager there," Tom requested.

A few moments later he was talking with the official. After the man was assured of the young inventor's identity, he gave him the desired information, which Tom relayed to Bud.

"Part of the *Spray Cloud*'s cargo was unimportant," he said. "But the rest would be a pirate's prize. It was uranium!"

"Uranium again!" Bud echoed.

Tom frowned. "Those pirates are doubtless planning more devilish raids, which might be carried out any moment. We'll have to hurry things along so we can get started on our hunt. Let's proceed with the Fat Man test," Tom urged. "It's getting late."

Leading the way, he hurried to the water-pressure tank. Beside it on a hand truck lay what looked like two prehistoric dinosaur eggs. Folded around them were thin, jointed pieces of metal. Tom picked up one of the suits, Bud the other.

"Your attention, folks!" Bud mimicked a circus barker. "Watch while we transform these Humpty Dumpties into men!"

He made a sweeping, magicianlike gesture as both boys unlocked the quartz window-doors. Then they climbed into the suits, and after quickly checking the mechanical devices, started to operate the controls. Slowly the pantograph arms and legs unfolded and moved into position. A few moments later the boys' audience beheld two grotesque creatures, standing upright, their attached fingers and toes giving them an uncanny human appearance.

When the Fat Men began to walk, the onlookers grinned at their peculiar waddling gait. Reaching the tank, which was filled with salt water, Tom and Bud jumped in. They bobbed around for several seconds, then began to descend.

The Fat Men were ready for the test

The lid of the tank was closed and Baker slowly turned on the pressure. The watchers, recalling Tom's frightful experience before in this same tank, waited intently. Baker, kneeling at a glass peephole in the lid, turned on the underwater light and watched. The boys were slowly walking around on the bottom, apparently untroubled as the pressure increased beyond what anyone had ever withstood and remained alive.

"Where's the oxygen hose?" Sandy asked.

"Everything's inside the Fat Man," Baker replied. "It's not dependent on outside help. But you'll see air bubbles come out of the top."

"Tell me something more about the principle of the escape suit," Mrs. Swift said, smiling proudly at another of her son's accomplishments.

"The lithium hydroxide," said Baker, "is taking care of what the boys are exhaling. And that excellent gadget by which Tom is getting oxygen from the water is a great invention, harder to perfect than the sub itself. If anything should happen to the jetmarine, they would be able to live in the suits a long time."

The period for the test was up and Baker slowly reduced the pressure. Finally the lid of the tank was opened. The two Fat Men bobbed to the surface and were helped from the water by several willing pairs of hands.

Again the boys' audience smiled as Tom and Bud awkwardly emerged from the suits. It took them several minutes to do so, but Tom had asked that they be given no assistance unless it was absolutely necessary.

"Say, where's Chow?" Tom looked around. "I thought he wanted to watch this test."

"He sure did," said Bud. "What became of him after his phone call?"

No one knew the whereabouts of the Texan and decided that something very urgent must have taken him away, since the cook was always eager to watch Tom's inventions at work.

To Chow the call had been important and grew more so as the minutes passed. After leaving the boys, he had boarded a bus for mid-town Shopton at the urgent call of his friend Gus Miller who owned a diner.

Gus's regular chef, it seemed, had gone home sick and Chow had promised to help out during the rush hour. Besides this, the man had told Chow he had twice overheard two customers talking in low tones about Tom Swift. It might be well to look them over if they should come in.

"I'll sure do that, and besides, I can slap hamburgers as fast as the next one!" Chow grinned.

The cook arrived at the diner to find Gus dashing about like a human octopus, frying eggs, waiting on the counter, and ringing the cash register all at the same time. The tall, skinny man's Adam's apple bobbed with delight when he saw his friend.

"Hop to it, Chow," he said, pointing to the kitchen in the rear. "Mulligan stew's the special today. It's popular. Better make some more."

Chow whipped an apron about his rotund middle, set a white hat jauntily on the back of his bald head, and grinned.

"Yell your orders loud enough for me to hear 'em in the galley, Gus," he said.

"Don't have to," the owner replied, hooking his thumbs into his suspenders. "I got this newfangled gimmick yesterday." He pointed to a small mike concealed under the far end of the counter. "I just whisper into this," he said, "an' it comes out right over the stove. Go listen!"

As Chow retreated to the back room, Gus strode to the end of the counter. "One on a raft!" he said softly. His words echoed in the kitchen, and Chow's eyes widened.

"Real modern," the cook approved. "I'll have to tell Tom about this."

For the next hour the team of Gus and Chow served a stream of hungry customers. The pot of mulligan stew was nearly empty when the perspiring Chow suddenly heard some strange words over the loud-speaker.

"We'll do this Swift job and get out of here," a man said.

"When?" came another voice.

"*Shhh!* Not so loud."

Chow was so startled he dropped his ladle into the steaming gravy and hurried out to the counter. Two rough-looking men were seated near the hidden mike. Chow approached them.

"Did I hear you mention Tom Swift?" he asked.

The two customers looked at each other in surprise. Then the taller one sneered and said, "No, we didn't, skinhead! I jest told my pal here we have a job to finish swift—in a hurry. Catch? Now scram back to your hamburgers!"

"Wait!" said the other man. "We might as well pay snoopy here and leave." He reached into his pocket and pulled out a handful of change, which he slapped on the counter.

Among the quarters, dimes, and nickels was a dog's-head coin!

CHAPTER 11

THE MYSTERIOUS PRISONER

WHEN HE saw the dog's-head coin on the counter, Chow, who had learned from Tom the story of the Cuban peso, was thunderstruck. He made a grab for it.

"Hey, not so fast!" the taller man rasped, as he retrieved the strange coin. At the same time he reached over and gave Chow a push. The portly cook teetered back into a rack of stacked cups, sending them to the floor in a crashing cascade.

Gus rushed to his friend's side and tried to grab Chow's assailant. But the two men slipped quickly from their stools and headed for the door, their fists cocked. As they stepped out, however, they ran square into a young policeman about to enter the diner for lunch.

"Hold it!" the officer demanded, sensing something was wrong.

But the pair had no intention of heeding the warning. Both made a bolt for freedom, almost knocking the officer off his feet.

"Stop 'em!" Chow yelled. "They're pirates!"

"Halt!" the officer shouted, running after them.

The short man disappeared down a back alley and escaped, but the policeman flung himself on the back of the taller man, dragging him to the ground. After snapping handcuffs on his prisoner, the officer marched him back to the diner.

"What's this about pirates?" the policeman demanded.

Then amid excitement and hubbub from the other diners, who rushed over, Chow related his suspicions.

"I ain't done nothing," the prisoner protested as he was led away to headquarters.

Chow immediately telephoned to Tom. After telling the young inventor what had happened, Chow warned, "Brand my six shooter, but I think there's a big gang around Shopton what's out to get you, Tom."

"Thanks, Chow. I'll be careful. Right now, I'm going down to headquarters."

Tom was eager to get a look at the man who possessed the dog's-head coin. He drove speedily to headquarters and raced up the granite steps in front of the building three at a time. When he told the desk sergeant why he was there, the officer ushered Tom into the cell block.

"The man says his name's Trebar," the sergeant said as they walked along. "He's in the next cell."

Tom immediately recognized the prisoner. He was the man whom Dansitt had picked up in his plane!

"Sergeant," Tom said excitedly, "this man is friendly with a guy named Dansitt who nearly ran me down with a plane."

Trebar scowled as Tom queried, "Where did Dansitt take you that day?"

The prisoner turned to the officer. "Do I have to answer this kid's questions?"

"You'd better. Several people have asked the police to find Dansitt. If you tell us where he is, it may go easier with you." Then the officer nodded to Tom. "Go ahead. Question him."

"Where did Dansitt take you?" Tom pressed.

The man sat back on his bunk, lit a cigarette, and gave a half-smirk. "Okay, I'll tell all," he said.

Tom exchanged glances with the officer, who called a police stenographer to note down what Trebar was about to say. When a young man with pad and pencil arrived, Trebar said:

"I'm a stunt man at a circus. I sit on flagpoles. But I don't like to climb flagpoles. So Mr. Dansitt flies me over the flagpoles and I drop down on top of 'em."

With that he blew out a cloud of smoke and laughed raucously.

The sergeant flushed with anger. "Cut out the cracks. Tell us the story straight!" he warned. "Is Dansitt a friend of yours?"

The prisoner looked insolently from Tom to the

sergeant. "Of course he's a friend of mine. And he'll get me out of this jam, too. A guy can have friends, can't he?"

Tom took up his questioning again. "Where did you get that dog's-head coin the cook saw?"

"That chowderhead needs glasses," the man replied. "I don't have a peso."

"I didn't say it was a peso," Tom said, as Trebar purpled at his own blunder. "Where is it?"

The man reluctantly pulled it from his pocket.

"Where did you get it, from Dansitt? Is it the insigne of your gang?"

"I found it!" Trebar shouted. "There's no law against finding things! I keep it for a souvenir!"

The officer whispered to Tom that he thought further interrogation was useless at this time. As he did, the prisoner stormed:

"You can't hold me!"

"You'll be fined for assaulting Chow," the sergeant reminded him.

"Okay, I'll pay the fine, but let me out of here!"

Tom took the officer aside, and after a conversation in low tones, the police sergeant turned to the prisoner.

"We're going to hold you a few days for investigation."

"You can't!" Trebar shouted. "I'll get my lawyer!"

"That's your privilege," the sergeant said as he and Tom left the cell block. Turning to Tom, he added, "We'll let you know what we find out. I'll check the FBI records to see if this man is wanted."

The route back to the plant led past Gus's diner. Tom saw Chow coming out the door, a package under his arm, and stopped.

"Hey, Chow! Hop in. I'll drive you home."

"Okay, boss," the Texan replied, grinning. "An' here's somethin' for you—mulligan stew!"

"That's something I can eat any time," Tom said. "And by the way, between jobs for the Swifts, you might take up police work. You did a swell job having that fellow nabbed. He's a friend of Dansitt's, and no doubt one of the pirates."

"Well, brand my night stick!" the cook exclaimed. "I sure hope the *hombre* gets to talkin'."

After eating his lunch, Tom decided to have a complete check made of the men and gadgets which guarded Swift Enterprises. He ordered that the magnetized fence which surrounded it be looked over inch by inch. The radar equipment, warning of sky visitors, was to be thoroughly tested. He also made arrangements to have the number of night watchmen doubled. Tom himself erected a giant distorter on top of the laboratory building which was the tallest one on the grounds. He was satisfied that this precaution would effectively shield the Swift property from any possible blackout attacks by the pirates.

Later, he walked to the shed where the two-man submarine was undergoing last-minute work. Coming toward him was Baker, a broad smile on his face.

"Tom, there's not a sign of corrosion on the inside of that test jet engine you've had in the salt-water bath," he said. "That osmiridium you sprayed on the pipes did the trick. Someday let me know just how much osmium and how much iridium you used in the formula, will you?"

"Okay. I'll do that."

Tom was thrilled. Now he could keep the hydraulic jet engines of the submarine working indefinitely without the danger of corrosion from sea water. The young inventor had worked hard on this problem. He knew that even stainless-steel pipes would not hold up; that paint could not withstand the intense heat; and that rubber would insulate the sea water from the nuclear reactor and prevent good heat transference.

After figuring out the alloy osmiridium, Tom had distilled it into the jetmarine by a superhigh vacuum so that every exposed surface of the machinery was protected.

"We start our journey to the Atlantic at dawn tomorrow," Tom told the engineer enthusiastically. "Everything ready?"

"Yes. The men are all set."

"I want this to appear to be just an ordinary delivery job in the *Sky Queen*," Tom said. "Too much of a convoy would certainly attract attention and that's what we want to avoid."

"Good reasoning." Baker nodded. "Anyway, if those pirates try to steal the sub they'll have several of us to reckon with."

"Telephone for Mr. Swift Jr.!" came over the loud-speaker.

Tom hurried into the shed and picked up the receiver. The speaker was Mrs. Newton.

"I have news about Ned!" she exclaimed. "Two

men called here—the captain and the purser of the *Nantic*."

"What did they say?" Tom asked excitedly.

"Ned's alive but a prisoner. The—the men wouldn't come right out and say, but I think they believe his captors are trying to get him to reveal information about your secret inventions and plans, then—then kill him!" Mrs. Newton burst into tears. "Oh, Tom, we must do something quick!"

"We will!" Tom cried. "Please try to bear up. Bud and I will be ready to leave for the Caribbean day after tomorrow, and Dad has already gone to do what he can."

"We caught the guard unawares.

"Oh, that's so good to hear," Mrs. Newton said. "Tom, I almost forgot to tell you. I asked those men to come over and relate the whole story to you."

"I'll meet them at the gate."

Ten minutes later Tom was escorting the ship's officers to the waiting room in the gatehouse. They introduced themselves as Captain Wellman and Purser Hange.

"Everyone on the *Nantic* suddenly blacked out," the captain reported. "But Mr. Newton, Hange, and I came to almost at once. Several men were climbing over the ship's rail, and they began to go through the passengers' pockets."

That's how we escaped."

"By that time," Hange took up the story, "we three were sufficiently recovered to go after those pirates. We fought them all right until reinforcements arrived and then we were overpowered."

Tom was leaning forward eager to hear more. Captain Wellman said:

"As they dragged us to the rail, we were forced to inhale some stuff that knocked us out. When Hange and I regained consciousness, we found ourselves prisoners in an isolated cabin on the Florida coast. The place was patrolled continually by an armed guard."

"Another guy," the purser said, "brought us food and we overheard a little of what the two said. That's how we know about Mr. Newton."

"Have you any idea where he is?" Tom asked quickly.

"None. I once heard the guard say, 'They'll never find the Dog,' and I thought it might be a code or password."

"I believe it is," Tom said. "By the way, how did you manage to escape?"

The captain laughed. "The guy who brought our food got careless and we knocked him out. Then we escaped and caught the guard unawares!"

"Did you notify the police?" Tom asked.

"As soon as we could get to them," Hange answered. "The police went right out to the shack, but of course the men had skipped. We got in touch with the steamship office. When we learned Mr. Newton was still missing, we decided to come here and see his wife."

"Do you think the pirates use a sub for their raids?"

The men shrugged. They had seen nothing to indicate by what method the pirates had carried them to the shore.

"I guess we're lucky to be alive," Captain Wellman said, rising. "Well, good-by, Mr. Swift. If we get any more tips, we'll contact you."

Tom thanked the men and they left. Later, Tom and Bud met, had a bite to eat, and went to sleep in the lounge of the laboratory building to keep their whereabouts as secret as possible from their enemies. Just before dawn an alarm clock the young inventor had set buzzed insistently.

"Nearly time for the jetmarine to make her maiden voyage," Tom thought excitedly. "And the first trip is a pirate hunt!"

CHAPTER 12

A SUB IN THE SKY

IN THE DARK HOURS before dawn there was feverish activity at the Swift plant. The jetmarine, covered with a brown tarpaulin, was mounted onto a large twelve-wheel trailer and driven toward the underground hangar of Tom Swift's *Sky Queen*.

At the same time, Tom was holding a conference in his private office. The young inventor sat at his desk, with his chief engineers, several trusted workmen, and Bud Barclay gathered around him.

"This is a dangerous mission," Tom began. "Dansitt and his spies might try to wreck our plans to launch the jetmarine. I have no doubt they know in general what we are doing."

"Do you really think there's that much danger?" Bud asked skeptically.

"More than you think."

Arvid Hanson nodded in agreement.

"They know we're ready to move our atomic sub," Tom went on, "but there's one little item they don't know."

"What's that?" Bud asked eagerly.

Tom smiled. "How we're going to move it," he said. "That's where I hope to fool them."

Bud Barclay scratched his head and frowned. "You're going to truck it to Stillman's Wharf, aren't you?"

"That's what everybody thinks," Tom said. "And I hope our enemies think so too. I brought that special trailer in here in broad daylight."

"You mean you're not going to ship it by truck?" Bud looked incredulous, then he added, "I suppose you're going to put wings on it and fly it down to the ocean."

Hanson smiled. "Barclay, you're a budding genius."

Bud grinned. "Yeah, I know what you mean. All sap." Then he turned to Tom. "Just how *are* you going to get this thing to Stillman's?"

"It's simple," Tom said. "I'm going to load her onto the *Sky Queen*."

The murmur that arose from the men indicated they did not believe that Tom's atomic aircraft, powerful as it was, would lift the additional load of the submarine and the cranes which would lower it into dry dock.

"I know what you're all thinking," he said, "but I've figured it out."

Tom reached down to open his desk drawer. Pulling out a sheaf of papers covered with figures, he handed them to Hanson.

"How do these seem to you, Arv?"

The engineer looked intently at the figures, turning over page after page slowly.

"I guess you're right, Tom. The *Sky Queen*'s motors generate enough energy to carry our sub."

As Tom rose and moved toward the door, the others followed him.

"I have a trick up my sleeve," the young inventor said. "I'm going to try it before we roll the sub into the hangar of the *Sky Queen*."

As the others listened, their eyes grew wide and grins spread over their faces. Tom explained that he had had a dummy framework hastily constructed. Covered with canvas, it would look very much like the jetmarine.

"I'm going to mount that on the trailer and send her out in a few minutes," Tom said. "If the pirate gang is as watchful as I think it is, they'll be lying in ambush for it somewhere along the route. Meanwhile, the *Sky Queen* will be on her way to Stillman's Wharf with the real McCoy."

Tom led the way to the plant's huge carpentry shop, where the dummy jetmarine lay ready for its journey.

"There's only one thing bothering me," Bud said. "Who's going to drive this trailer?"

"Nobody's going to drive it," Tom said.

"I don't get it, genius boy," Bud remarked. He grabbed his head in his hands. "Come, nurse, put me in a strait jacket and take me to the booby hatch!"

Tom walked across the floor of the building to a small motor scooter and beckoned to Bud. "Here's how we're going to do it, pal. I've mounted a set of controls in the scooter. By manipulations, they'll drive the truck just the same as if someone were in it."

The inventor went on to explain how he had already trained one of his mechanics to ride behind the trailer and operate it by remote control. He had received special permission from the police chief to do this.

"And we're just about ready to go," Tom said, beckoning to the man he had selected for the risky assignment. "Are you all set, Jeffers?" he asked as a young man in white coveralls approached him.

"Okay, boss." Jeffers mounted the motor scooter and putted out of the building.

Meanwhile, the atomic submarine, at Tom's direction, had been lifted off the truck by a giant crane and lay alongside the underground hangar. Jeffers deftly manipulated the trailer into the building where the mock model was housed. A dozen workmen lifted the tarpaulin-covered object onto the vehicle.

"You'll exit through the main gate," Tom said to Jeffers.

A dummy driver was put into the trailer's seat and, with the motor scooter chugging some hundred feet behind, the vehicle glided through the grounds and out the main gate of Swift Enterprises.

"What will we do now?" Bud asked, as he and Tom saw the massive plant gates click shut.

"First, I'll phone the police to follow Jeffers," he said. "Then we'll wait and see what happens. Jeffers has a radio and will keep us informed."

After Tom had contacted the Shopton police, the boys hurried to the underground hangar. Tom beamed his electronic key on the hidden lock, and the door swung open silently.

"Hop to it, men," Tom said, beckoning his ground crew.

Ten minutes later the gleaming *Sky Queen* rose on the huge elevator from her underground nesting place to ground level. The portable cranes quickly attached themselves to the jetmarine, and as Tom directed the operation, the workers slid the atomic sub into the hangar in the aft section of the great aircraft.

"It's easy when you know how," Bud said admiringly.

The words were hardly off his tongue when Tom began to get a signal on his pocket radio.

"T for tomato, T for tomato," came the call.

"Okay," Tom answered. "What's going on?"

"Something fishy," Jeffers replied. "We're ten miles out. A car has just pulled up ahead of the trailer and another in back of it. They are forcing the trailer to the side of the road. I'm dropping behind a way. Shall I stop it?"

"Okay," Tom said. "Guide her to the side of the road and park. Tell me what's happening."

By this time several of Tom's trusted workers were crowded around him, listening to Jeffers' report of the attack on the mock submarine.

"Just as I thought," Tom said to his companions.

Then the voice of Jeffers came over louder. "Tom, two men have jumped out of each car. They have slugged the dummy driver. They're pulling off the tarpaulin. Oh!"

There was a slight pause. "Are they mad! They're cursing you from here to the Pacific!"

Tom chuckled. "Go on!"

"They seem confused as to how the truck was run. A couple of them are hurrying away from it as if they had seen a ghost. Here come the police," Jeffers said. "But I'm afraid they're too late. Those thugs took off in an awful hurry!"

"Good work, Jeffers," Tom said. "Get back here as quickly as you can. We'll pick up the trailer and the police report later." Then he turned to his men. "Now's the time for us to go," he said. "We've cleared the way. Everybody ready?"

He and Bud mounted the ladder which extended up to the height of two stories to the side of the giant aircraft.

"Where's Chow?" Tom remarked.

"You don't have to ask where I am," came a voice from inside the big ship. "Your ole chuck-wagon cook's been waitin' an hour. Ever since you phoned your family good-by."

When Tom was in the pilot's seat, he switched on the intercom and talked to crewmen in the rear of his plane. As soon as everything was ready, Tom signaled for two tractors to pull him far out on the take-off strip. When this had been done, he cleared everybody back from the sides of the ship. Then he applied the atomic power. With a whistling roar the *Sky Queen* rose vertically into the air.

"You sure were right, Tom," Bud said. "This ship handles the jetmarine like she was a toy."

After they had gained ten thousand feet altitude, Tom applied forward thrust and the plane headed for its destination. Within half an hour the dim grayness of the ocean came into view.

"We're almost there," Bud chuckled, "and believe me, the sooner we get this precious baby down in dry dock the better."

Tom looked through his electronic-prismed binoculars to the ground below. Choosing a level place on the beach near Stillman's, he eased the *Sky Queen* down.

Several hundred feet above the ground, Bud, who had been inspecting the sub's equipment, burst into the cabin.

"Tom!" he cried. "What goops we are!"

"What's the matter?"

"The Fat Men—our escape suits—we left them at the plant!"

CHAPTER 13

A JET RESCUE

AS BUD flopped into the copilot's seat Tom looked at him in amazement.

"The Fat Men! Of all the things to forget! We shouldn't make a test run without them." Then, calming down, he added, "I'll have somebody fly them out in one of our jets."

Tom kept the *Sky Queen* hovering over Stillman's Wharf while he radioed home. Getting Baker out of bed, Tom asked him to have the escape suits sent as quickly as possible.

"The nearest airport to this place that'll accommodate a jet is one called Henley Field," Tom said. "It's ten miles from here. We'll pick the Fat Men up at noontime. Bud will drive over in a truck."

"I'll attend to it right away," Baker promised. "Good-by."

Tom eased the giant ship slowly toward the beach. The advance crew which Tom had sent to the wharf

105

came scurrying from a Quonset hut to watch the mammoth ship make her landing.

The Flying Lab came down perfectly, her jet lifters roaring. Tom cut the motors, taxied up to the dock, and climbed out, followed by Arv Hanson who would fly the *Sky Queen* back to Shopton.

"Shall we unload immediately, Tom?" one of the men asked.

"The quicker the better. We'll get the jetmarine into the dry dock and slap on that camouflage before people are awake."

Tom looked over the site for his secret launching. The inlet had been selected after several months of scouting by Hank Sterling and Arvid Hanson. They had surveyed shore-line localities and had come up with Stillman's as the perfect spot.

The boat yard, with a fine dry dock, had been abandoned as a Navy speedboat experimental center several years before. Now it had reverted to Mr. Stillman, the original owner. He lived on the property and puttered with small motorboats.

Under the new arrangement with Swift Enterprises, Mr. Stillman permitted Tom's construction engineers to ready the place as they pleased, which they had done in a matter of hours.

The young inventor watched with satisfaction as cranes deftly slid the atomic submarine from the hangar of the plane, swung it across the sand, and cradled the jetmarine in the dry dock.

At this moment the camouflage crew sprang into action. A few minutes later Bud cried admiringly:

"Jumping jets! That covering looks just like a strip of seashore."

"Right," Tom agreed. "Any roving pirate will miss it."

Tom spent the balance of the morning checking vital parts on his submarine. At eleven o'clock he dispatched Bud to the local airport.

"I think we've thrown the pirates off our trail," the young inventor said, "but we won't take any chances. Baker said he'd pack the Fat Men in boxes. They'll probably look like big refrigerator cartons. Somebody at the field will help you load them on the truck."

"Don't I get an escort?" Bud asked, giving Tom a slant-eyed look.

"I'm afraid that would arouse suspicion," the young inventor replied.

"Okay, pal. Now I'm in the trucking business." Bud saluted and strode off.

The copilot walked to the paved road about a quarter of a mile from Stillman's. A short distance beyond he stopped at Smitty's garage and rented a truck. The day was sunny and warm, and Bud enjoyed the ride through the scrub-pine country toward the small airport.

Arriving there, he pulled up beside the administration building and entered its tiny office. After introducing himself to the airport manager, Bud said he was awaiting a consignment from the Swift Construction Company.

"It'll be here soon," replied the man, a short, slender fellow with a blond mustache. "The pilot has radioed for clearance."

Bud did not have long to wait. Ten minutes later he caught the whistle and whine of a jet. Bud looked up, shading his eyes.

"Hey, what's the idea?" he said, squinting. "Why did they send two planes?"

The manager glanced skyward. "You're right. There are two jets. But the other pilot hasn't asked for landing directions."

Bud said no more, but he was worried. Had someone followed the Enterprises plane? Bud asked for a field glass and trained it on the strange ship. It seemed to bear no identification marks! A moment later the plane was out of sight.

"That's funny," Bud thought. "Well, I'll get out of here in a hurry before that guy does decide to land."

The Swifts' jet, after sweeping in an arc over the field, touched the earth lightly and rolled to a stop within a few feet of where Bud was waiting with the airport manager.

A young pilot grinned as he stepped from the plane. "FM at your service," he said, giving Bud a wink. "You guys would have forgotten your heads if they weren't riveted to your collarbones."

Bud grimaced. "I left one of my heads home as it was."

Amid good-natured needling the pilot and Bud hauled the two crates out of the jet and carried them to the truck.

"Who was that other throttle jockey upstairs with you?" Bud asked.

"I don't know. I didn't notice him until about a hundred miles back."

"Well, the FM are ready for the JM," Bud said, as the airport manager looked on wonderingly. "Now we're all set."

The jet pilot waved, stepped into his plane, and with a resounding *whoosh* zoomed back toward Shopton. Bud climbed into the cab of the truck, slammed the door, and started off with his cargo.

Back at Stillman's, meanwhile, Tom waited for Bud to return. The hands of the clock moved around to twelve, and when they approached one, the young inventor became concerned.

He hurried into the dock office and telephoned the airport. The manager said that Bud had left an hour before.

"He should have returned here half an hour ago," Tom said, a frown of worry creasing his forehead. Then, in order to double check, Tom radioed his office in Shopton. The jet pilot was nearly halfway home after making his delivery. Tom contacted him directly, and when he heard the story about the pursuing jet plane, he became more alarmed than ever.

Had one of his enemies followed and radioed word to henchmen to attack Bud's truck?

Tom hurried along the beach to where his crew was giving the *Sky Queen* a once-over. He raced up the ladder and into the plane.

"What's your hurry, boss?" Chow asked.

"More dirty work," Tom said. "Get set for a ride."

The pilot made his way forward to the nose of the plane and took his seat. Then he gave orders over the intercom for a quick take-off.

The plane roared into the air and in a few seconds Tom was over the small airport. Hovering stationary at ten thousand feet, he scanned the terrain below with his binoculars. Back and forth his gaze swept across the sandy pine-studded countryside.

Suddenly, at one end of a long swath of meadowland which bordered a creek, he spotted a plane and a truck. Tom intensified the magnification of his binoculars and the scene below was brought as close to him as if it had been ten feet away.

Could it be Bud's truck? But his friend was not in sight!

A moment later two men jumped from the back of the truck. One was Sidney Dansitt! Together, they began to lug a large crate toward the plane.

Tom, realizing he must act instantly, hit upon a daring plan. He shot acceleration into his jet motors for a dive. At terrific speed the *Sky Queen* wailed toward the meadow like a stricken banshee. Tom skimmed his enemies. The hot blast of the jets knocked Dansitt and his henchman to the ground. By the time they had a chance to glance up, the *Sky Queen* was a mile away.

Tom looked down at the two figures, who lay still for a moment. Then the men made a dash for their plane, dragging the crate.

Again the *Sky Queen* hurtled earthward. This

time the ship came so close to Dansitt's plane that its wings rocked in the backwash. As Tom zoomed upward again, the men dropped the crate and streaked for the plane. Much as he hated to let the men take off, Tom had no alternative at the present time. His chief concern was Bud's safety.

He eased the giant aircraft to the field alongside the truck, climbed down, and ran to the truck. Bud lay on the floor of the cab, trussed up and gagged. Tom released him and asked what had happened.

"Wow!" Bud said. "I sure fell for that trick!"

Then he told how he had run into a bank of fog, which he now suspected had been artificially made.

"I had to slow down to a crawl," he said, "and that's when they jumped me. Did they get our escape suits?"

When Tom explained how he had driven the thieves off, Bud remarked with a grin, "You certainly singed Dansitt's tail feathers."

"Not for long, probably," Tom replied. "That guy's hard to keep out of circulation."

Tom got into the *Sky Queen* and escorted the co-pilot, driving the truck below, to Stillman's Wharf. There they unloaded the escape suits and put them aboard the jetmarine. Then Tom telephoned the local township police chief, George Slater. Pledging the man to secrecy, he told him briefly of his mission at Stillman's Wharf and of the attack on Bud Barclay.

"I understand," Slater replied. "We'll get on the job right away."

The officer promised that he would keep a sharp

lookout for anyone answering Dansitt's description and would let Tom know immediately of any developments. No word came during the afternoon, however.

In the evening Tom reviewed with Bud the intricate handling of the submarine. Standing before the myriad-lighted control panel, Tom said finally:

"Enough for now, pal, or we'll see blinking lights in our dreams. Come on topside. Let's hit the sack."

"Not me," Bud protested. "I'm sleeping right here —baby sitter for your brain child." He stroked the periscope handle and grinned.

"Okay, if you want to," Tom replied. "I'm sleeping in the shack so I can be near the radio—just in case."

"*Adios!*"

When Tom arrived at the Quonset hut he dispatched two men to guard the property. After posting one lookout on the beach and the other offshore in a skiff, Tom felt that he had set up reasonable security. Both men, equipped with pocket radios tuned to Tom's receiver, were instructed to awaken him if they saw anything suspicious.

Tom kicked off his shoes and sat on the edge of the bunk. Except for the steady breathing of the other men sleeping in the hut, it was just as quiet inside as out. So far, things had gone well, Tom thought. His enemies had been shaken off, or at least they had lost the trail. He stretched out on the bunk and in a short time was asleep.

Soon after midnight the guard in the skiff detected

An earth-shaking explosion illuminated the shore

a shadow, moving silently along the shore past the wide inlet. The fragment of moon that hung low in the sky threw enough light across the inlet to reveal the knifelike hull of a lurking submarine.

"Tom Swift!" the startled guard radioed. "I see a—"

The warning was cut short by an earth-shaking explosion as a crimson flash illuminated the shore.

CHAPTER 14

THE SHAKEDOWN RUN

THE GROUND under the Quonset hut shook as if it had been caught in the fierce anger of an earthquake. Tom and his friends were knocked from their beds by the concussion.

Had the jetmarine exploded?

"What happened? Anybody hurt?" the men cried out.

"No," came a chorus of replies, but none of them knew the cause of the explosion.

"Follow me!" Tom ordered, grabbing a powerful spotlight. "The jetmarine! Oh, I hope Bud—"

As Tom ran frantically ahead of the others, he explained that he had heard a few cryptic words from the guard's radio, then the man had been cut off.

Tom's light stabbed the darkness as he reached the dry dock which was only three hundred yards away. Beaming his flash on the camouflaged covering of the submarine he cried out:

"Thank goodness the explosion wasn't here."

Hank Sterling clicked on a floodlight atop a nearby pole. The yellow glow spread over a wide area. As the group fanned out to investigate further, Tom peered beneath the camouflage. Bud was just coming out of the escape hatch.

"You okay?" Tom asked.

"Yes. What caused the explosion? The sub rocked like crazy and I was thrown out of my bunk."

"We don't know yet," Tom said grimly.

At this moment the guard who had been stationed on the beach ran up excitedly.

"Come quick!" he shouted. "Someone's crying for help in the surf."

The three raced in the direction toward which he was pointing.

"I'll bet it's the man I stationed in the boat," Tom said. "The blast probably knocked him out of it."

He and Bud could now hear the anguished cries of the struggling swimmer. They plunged into the surf and in a few minutes were beside the bobbing head of the guard.

"I'll tow him in," Bud offered, and with powerful strokes guided the man toward the beach.

The boys carried him out of reach of the combers and waited a few moments until the man could catch his breath.

"What happened?" Tom asked him.

The guard related that he had seen a prowling submarine. He had just started to broadcast a warning to Tom when he had been hurled from the skiff by the backwash of the explosion.

"Did you see where the blast was?" Bud asked eagerly.

"Yes," the man replied, pointing up the shore. "It hit there."

"I'll go up pronto," Bud offered.

"And I'll go with you," Tom declared, "as soon as we get this chap back to the hut." The swimmer was shaking like a leaf from his cold plunge.

The two boys carried the man to the hut, arriving just as a squad car pulled up. Police Chief Slater and another officer hopped out. Tom introduced himself and Bud.

The police chief was excited. "I thought we might get some fireworks around here after what you told me yesterday," he said. "But I didn't expect an atomic bomb! Where was the explosion?"

Tom told him that it was down the shore a short distance and led the way. In a few minutes they came to the mouth of a narrow reed-filled creek. As Tom stared into it, he noted that black mud had been spattered all over the banks.

"The explosion must have happened here!" he called, spotting a gaping hole in the creek bank.

The tidewater had run in and filled up the bottom of the gap. Scattered about were innumerable shrapnellike pieces of metal. Getting closer, the three saw a large piece that had some markings on it. Bud read aloud:

" 'MARK VI MOD. 3 U. S. NAVAL TORPEDO.'

"This is crazy!" he exclaimed. "Our own Navy firing torpedoes at us!"

Tom examined it, saying, "I'll bet this was never fired by the Navy. The pirates shot it to get the jetmarine and missed!"

"But where did they get a Navy torpedo?" Bud asked.

"The Navy loses lots of them during their practice firing," the police chief replied.

"Boy, they sure must want to destroy the jetmarine bad," Bud said. "Those torpedoes cost over a hundred thousand dollars and the chances of finding a stray one are mighty slim."

"But the ones that are found aren't equipped with war heads," the police chief pointed out.

Tom suggested that if the pirates had a scientist who could invent a blackout ray he would have been able to rig up an explosive charge for an empty torpedo shell which the pirates might have found.

The group returned to the hut, and Chief Slater put in a phone call to the Coast Guard. After a few minutes' conversation he hung up and reported to the boys that a radar-equipped motor launch would be sent out at once to patrol the area.

"If that sub surfaces, they'll find it," the police chief predicted.

He offered to remain at Stillman's to help guard the spot. Tom thanked him for the offer, but said he felt sure that the enemy would not dare attempt another attack that night.

"If something does go wrong, we'll let you know in a hurry, though," he added.

"Right. We'll be on tap," Slater said, and departed with the other officer in the squad car.

Tom's crew urged the two boys to get some sleep but this proved to be impossible to do. Both Tom and Bud tossed restlessly until dawn. Finally Tom arose and hurried out to the jetmarine, near which Bud was pacing up and down.

"Bud," he said, joining his friend, "I have an idea. Let's assume that it was the pirate sub firing in here. Suppose she's not an atomic sub. The jetmarine could beat her to the base on Spaniel Island with ease —be there waiting for her!"

"Terrific idea!" Bud agreed. "When do we leave?"

"Within an hour," Tom replied. "By the way, I've plotted a course that will take us right over the *Spray Cloud*'s approximate position."

"Why?" Bud asked.

"I want to prove that the pirates did this job. When I phoned the North-South Atlantic office, the traffic manager said that the uranium was stowed in hold Number Four."

"Aft of midships?"

"Yes."

Chow prepared breakfast for them. As they were finishing, the cook answered the ringing telephone.

"It's for you, Tom," he said.

The caller was Chief Slater. "I've just picked up some news on the police teletype," he said.

"What is it?" Tom asked.

"Day before yesterday a fellow named Dansitt was arrested in a small town below here for speeding," Slater began. "The car was owned by the passenger, George Jennig, a Florida lawyer. After we heard from you we alerted other stations."

"Where's Dansitt now?" Tom asked excitedly.

"I don't know. But let me tell you the rest of the story. He and Jennig paid their fine and were let off. But this morning at four o'clock the same car was found abandoned near a beach on the ocean south of here. There's no trace of the men."

"So you think it's possible that they might have been picked up by a sub?" Tom asked, his heart pounding.

"Exactly!" Slater answered. "Be pretty hard to locate them now. But a guard's being set near their car. If they come for it, they'll be taken into custody."

Tom hung up, but a moment later was asking the long-distance operator to connect him with Admiral Hopkins in Washington.

Screening his conversation as best he could from any eavesdroppers on the line, the inventor told the officer what had happened in the past few hours and of his own plan to take a look at the suspected islands.

"I'd appreciate having your patrol stay away from the immediate area," Tom requested. "But near enough for me to call on them if I need help. I want to have a try at rescuing my uncle, Ned Newton, without having the pirates aware I'm around," he explained.

"Good enough. I'll arrange things as you wish," the admiral promised. "Good luck, Tom!"

Half an hour later Tom and Bud were ready for their voyage and hastened to the submarine. To their surprise, Chow had arranged for a christening.

He stood with a large bottle of ginger ale in his hand, a broad grin on his face.

"This lil ole sub's got to have a name," he announced. "How's the *Sea Dart* sound to you, Tom? The jetmarine's fast as an arrow, an' brand my shootin' range, I'll bet she hits the bull's-eye every time."

"It's a swell name," Tom replied.

The other onlookers approved also and Chow handed the bottle to Tom. But the young inventor, smiling, returned it and said:

"You do the christening, Chow."

Proudly the cook stood by as Tom and Bud shook hands with everyone and climbed aboard. Bud disappeared down the hatch to the control room. The lines were thrown off and the atomic submarine was ready to start her maiden voyage.

"I christen thee the *Sea Dart*," Chow murmured in awe and cracked the bottle on the stern.

The others clapped and Hank Sterling shouted, "Success, Tom! Smoke out those pirates!"

The jetmarine instantly betrayed her great power in a fast, easy getaway from the inlet. A mile out in the ocean, Tom, unable to wait any longer, said:

"Bud, shall we take her down for the first underwater run?"

"I'd hate to try stopping you!" Bud laughed, and moved forward to the heavy transparent nose to get a fish's-eye view of the submersion. As the submarine began to descend, he cried out:

"This is super, Tom! With that bright sun on the surface, I can see way ahead!"

For minutes Bud stood fascinated, watching schools of mackerel, blues, and other coastal fish scoot through the yellow-green water as the *Sea Dart* passed by them.

"I'm going to give her a high-speed run right now!" Tom called, and Bud quickly joined his friend midships.

A quick release of the cadmium rods and the jetmarine shot ahead. Tom's hand moved slowly forward against the second bank of rods. Faster and faster and with no vibration the *Sea Dart* picked up momentum.

The speed indicator went higher and higher. Finally Bud exclaimed, "This is almost twice as fast as anyone has traveled underseas before!"

Tom's face creased into a pleased grin.

After sustaining the same speed for fifteen minutes, he said:

"Now comes the most important test. She's passed her first dive and underwater run. But how will she surface?"

As Tom inched the gear to the *Up* position, a look of strained anticipation appeared on the two adventurers' faces.

CHAPTER 15

UNDERSEA FIREWORKS

WITH THE SAME smooth performance that she had shown in her dive, the atomic sub responded to her young skipper's control and nosed upward in a seemingly effortless glide.

"What a dream!" Bud murmured enthusiastically. "I can hardly wait now to take her out into really deep water so that we can submerge to where no man has ever been."

"Yes," Tom replied, "I even hope to solve the mystery of the phantom bottom."

Bud scratched his head and was about to query Tom when the young inventor continued:

"But first we have to locate the *Spray Cloud*."

"Aye, aye, skipper," Bud replied.

"We're heading directly to the X marks on our chart. We should be there before too long."

As the *Sea Dart* skimmed along slightly below the

surface, Tom found time to explain certain things to his friend which he had not mentioned before.

"We've built all the features of the Barton bathysphere into this craft," he said. "Beebe first used it in 1934 to go down three thousand feet. And we applied the principles of the benthoscope that Barton used to descend forty-five hundred feet in 1949."

"But they weren't submarines," Bud commented.

Tom smiled. "That's right. Even though our task is more difficult, we'll still go down farther!"

"That's a bit over my head," Bud joked. Then he added, "What's all that strange-looking gear up in the bow, Tom?"

"Sorry I didn't have time to explain it to you, old man," Tom replied. "It belongs to a friend of Dad's —an oceanographer who asked me to do some research for his society."

"Sounds kind of highbrow," Bud returned.

"Not at all. They're just a group of hardheaded scientists who want facts and I propose to bring back a bushel."

"No oysters?"

"Another crack like that and I'll lay you right on the half shell," Tom said. "But seriously, that metal case you saw forward is a deep-water camera. The contraptions on the side are connected to the suction nets that are rigged outside the hull."

"Suction nets?" Bud looked incredulous. "I thought they were intake ports."

"In a way they are," Tom explained. "In them I hope to catch the fast underwater species of deep-sea fish that always escape the slow-moving nets of scientists."

"You suck them right in?" Bud queried.

"That's the idea."

Bud shook his head up and down and grinned. "That's what I get for being the friend of a genius," he said. "And is that other thing—a gun?"

"Not the kind you think," Tom replied, and reminded his friend that the Swifts were always opposed to arming any of their craft, and preferred to outwit their enemies by strategy rather than bloodshed.

"It's an electronic oscillator ray gun," Tom explained, smiling. "It works only under water, and is designed to kill predatory sea creatures."

"It won't work topside?"

"No. It's harmless against human beings once we surface."

As the *Sea Dart* slid through the water toward her destination, Bud became thoughtful. After a few minutes he said:

"I've heard that deep-sea squid attack six-ton whales. I'm mighty relieved to know we have this oscillator gimmick."

Tom smiled and glanced at him. "Did you know that tentacle squids are jet-propelled just like this sub?"

"No. I've never met any squids. I belong to a different fraternity," Bud replied, laughing.

"Well, by blowing out a fast stream of water through a siphon which also serves as a rudder,"

Tom explained, "the squids can scoot and dodge at a great pace."

"Good boys for infighting," Bud said. "Okay, skipper, we're almost there."

He handed Tom a chart which the young scientist studied for a few minutes.

"The *Spray Cloud*'s down nine hundred feet on a rock shelf. If this oceanographic survey is correct, we ought to hit the *Spray Cloud* right on the button."

Tom switched on a powerful undersea light, cut the speed of the *Sea Dart,* and started gradual descent toward the spot where the stricken ship had been reported sinking.

"Run up forward and look out," Tom instructed Bud. "Let me know the minute you see anything."

Bud squeezed along the narrow catwalk that led to the bow of the jetmarine. As he looked out along the swath of light which cut through the darkening sea, he could see myriads of colored fish and strange sea plants.

Suddenly the hull of a ship loomed up in the path of light.

"Hold it, Tom! There's something ahead."

The young inventor was at his friend's side immediately.

"I guess this is it all right," Tom said. "Can you make out the lettering on the bow?" he asked as he turned the beam slightly.

"It's our ship all right," Bud explained, and excitedly spelled out the letters "S-P-R-A-Y C-L-O-U-D! Nice navigating, mariner."

Tom maneuvered the submarine closer to the *Spray Cloud*.

"Take over the controls, will you?" he asked Bud. "I'm going to hop into one of the Fat Men and investigate this wreck. If the uranium is gone, it'll answer a lot of questions."

Tom wriggled into an escape suit. Then he stepped into the pressure chamber, released a sliding panel in the side of the submarine, and stepped out onto the ocean floor.

He waited breathlessly to see what the effect on the Fat Man would be. There was no apparent change. The young inventor sighed in relief and started propelling himself toward the dark hulk of the sunken vessel.

The *Spray Cloud* had settled stern first, and Tom walked underneath the upended bow. He switched on his sonarphone to report to Bud.

"This portside seems to be undamaged," he said. "I'll go around to starboard."

"Okay," Bud answered. "I'll bring the *Sea Dart* right along behind you."

Tom made his way underneath the bow, his undersea light casting an almost solid bar of illumination ahead of him. Reaching the other side of the ship, he played the light methodically along the hull. When he came amidships Tom found a gaping jagged-edged hole.

"Here it is!" Tom exclaimed. "There's an opening big enough to drive a truck through."

Tom turned around to see Bud peering through the transparent nose of the submarine.

"Wow, a direct torpedo hit!" Bud exclaimed.

"I don't think so," Tom replied, examining the ripped steel plates more closely. "The force of the blast was out, not in. If the pirates did it, they probably planted a bomb after the robbery."

"Where did you say the uranium was stored?"

"In Number Four hold, just aft of midships," Tom replied. "I'll head for there. Come along to release my cutting equipment, will you? I'll have to burn my way through."

Tom walked across the ocean floor until he came to the spot where he judged the uranium had been stowed. The submarine followed him, and Tom waited as a small door in the side of the *Sea Dart* slid open, revealing an oxyhydrogen cutting torch. Tom manipulated his pantograph arms and gripped the triple hose.

"Thanks, pal. Now we'll see some sparks fly."

Tom carried the undersea salvage tools to the side of the ship. Adjusting the nozzle, he started to cut. A fierce jet of flame bit into the steel as though it were soft pine wood.

Through one of the tubes came a steady blast of air to blow the water away, allowing the flame to do its clean, swift surgery. Tom cut out a rectangle the size of a garage door and stepped aside as he extinguished the cutting flame.

"Timber!" Bud cried, as the metal slab fell slowly outward onto the ocean bottom.

"Now I'll find out whether the uranium was the loot they were looking for," Tom remarked.

He set the tool against the side of the ship and stepped through the opening. As Bud watched Tom disappear inside the ghostly wreck a startled cry came over the sonarphone.

"Bud! Help! Quick!"

CHAPTER 16

AN OCEAN MONSTER

BUD BARCLAY'S BLOOD ran cold when he heard Tom's plea for help.

"Tom! Tom! What's the matter?"

There was no reply.

A clammy sweat broke out on Bud's forehead. He was at the bottom of the sea, virtually alone. His best friend was in trouble, perhaps fatally injured! Both Tom's life and the world's greatest invention were his responsibility! He must rescue Tom.

"Tom, hold on," Bud shouted into the mike. "Hold on as long as you can. I'll be right with you!"

After checking the instrument panel to be sure the submarine would remain stationary, Bud slipped into the other Fat Man and hastened to the special compression chamber. Then he climbed out onto the ocean bottom. The slow pace at which he had to approach the opening which Tom had cut in the side of the ship was maddening. But finally Bud made it.

The light from the escape suit's built-in torch shone into the ship's hold. Bud looked down. One of the pantograph arms of Tom's Fat Man stuck out from under a huge packing case!

Bud guessed what had happened. The force of the cutting tool had churned up the water inside the hold, and the large crate, which had probably been off balance, had fallen forward just as Tom entered, pinning him to the floor of the hold.

Bud extended his mechanical arms and pushed against the box. It moved slightly.

"Tom, Tom, can you hear me?" Bud shouted into his mike.

Still no reply. Bud worked furiously to move the obstruction which might be crushing the life out of his friend.

But he could not budge the case. His brain was in a turmoil. If Tom had to solve such a problem, what would he do?

"What would Tom do?" Bud kept repeating to himself.

Suddenly a thought occurred to him. Turning, Bud made his way out of the hold to the side of the ship, picked up the cutting tools, then went back into the ship. After adjusting the nozzle, Bud cut a hole in the bottom of the wooden box. Then he extinguished the flame and shot air into the huge box. It lifted an inch!

Instantly Bud put his shoulder against the case.

Then, using the control devices deftly, he shoved the burden off Tom.

It was then that Bud heard the most welcome sound of his life. A choking gasp came over his speaker.

Tom was alive!

Bud manipulated his pantograph arms to guide Tom's Fat Man to the *Sea Dart*. Once inside the compression chamber, between the outer and inner hulls, Bud equalized the pressure, then stumbled into the main section with his friend.

Quickly stripping off his Fat Man, Bud hastened to free Tom. He accomplished this in a few moments. The young inventor grinned in relief.

"Wow! That was a close one," he said. "Thanks for the rescue. My transmitter was kayoed."

"Looks like old Davy Jones doesn't like intruders." Bud managed a grin.

"He really conked me when I stepped inside the ship," Tom admitted. "But I'd better hurry back and take another look."

"Right now?"

"We've lost enough time already," Tom said.

"I think I'd better escort you this time," Bud suggested.

"All right. Let's go."

After a quick examination of his Fat Man, Tom found everything in good working order, except the transmitter, which they quickly repaired.

Soon the boys were on the ocean floor again, making their way through the opening in the side of the ship. After groping around inside, they finally reached the locker where the precious uranium had been stowed. Tom needed only a glance to see that the hold had been rifled.

"There's no question in my mind," said Tom, "but that the pirates are responsible for this job. There was so much uranium and it was so hard to get at that they couldn't remove it all before the crew revived."

"And," Bud added, "the pirates figured it was necessary to kill the crew and blow up the ship to destroy all the evidence. Ugh, it's horrible. Let's get out of here." Then, on second thought, he asked, "What about the crew? Should we look for them?"

"The sea life has mercifully taken care of them by now," Tom said quietly. "Too bad."

Once inside the submarine again, the boys refreshed themselves with a lunch from the food locker. As Tom finished a cup of hot chocolate, he said:

"We're only about fifty miles west of Lazar Canyon. It's four thousand feet deep at that point."

Bud munched a sandwich. "I get it," he said. "Our deep-sea fisherman is thinking of going down there."

Tom grinned. "You're looking into your crystal ball again, pal. I was just thinking the canyon might be a good spot to solve the problem of the phantom bottom."

"You mentioned that before," Bud said. "It sounds like something that might go right through to the other side of the world. What is this thing, anyway?"

Tom laughed. "Well, you asked for it, so here

goes. For several years, when fathometers on ships have been taking depth soundings, they often pick up a false bottom before getting the actual depth. This phantom bottom is like a mass that lies somewhere between the real bottom and the surface."

"What's the mass made of?"

"Some scientists say fish," Tom explained. "Others shrimp and still others squid. I'm a 'squid' man myself."

Bud looked blank but interested. "Why?"

"Because the phantom bottom can change its position in the span of one day from three hundred to eighteen hundred feet or more," Tom added.

"So?"

"The squid are better able than fish or shrimp to make this great shift," Tom answered. "Change in pressure doesn't bother them."

"I see," said Bud.

"With this sub," Tom went on, "we can go to any depth and find out for ourselves."

"You mean spend a little time with the fishes, then visit the shrimp and finally drop in on your favorites —the squids!"

Tom smiled. "To find out which family is on the level," he quipped.

Bud let out a sigh. "Okay, I'm with you."

The boys took their positions in the control room, and the *Sea Dart* began to plunge downward along the steep slope that falls away from the continental shelf.

"I think I'll use the fathometer to find out how deep it is here," Tom remarked.

He flicked the switch and instantly picked up two peculiar light patterns on the scope.

"For Pete's sake, what's going on?" Bud cried.

Tom scratched his head. "One of course is the depth—two thousand feet. Say, Bud," he cried excitedly, "I believe the other is the phantom bottom! Get the undersea television equipment out and take movies off the screen. Doing it this way, we can get both close-ups and panorama shots."

"At your service, Mr. Hollywood," Bud said, going into the nose of the submarine and swinging the camera into position.

The door to the control room was left open so that Tom could watch the proceedings. The *Sea Dart* moved slowly through the inklike ocean.

"I'm expecting some luminous squid," Tom said, snapping off the sub's lights.

As he spoke, a sudden sprinkling of tiny red and yellow lights in regular patterns appeared in the darkness ahead. Rows of glowing dots were gliding in all directions. Bud switched on the TV and movie camera.

"Look at those squids!" Bud cried. "They're as thick as mush."

Tom activated the suction nets to get some specimens. At the same time, the searchlight was turned on and more pictures taken.

"I guess that's enough," Tom said. "Now we'll follow the mass and see where it goes."

In a moment the school of squid began to drop like an elevator. The jetmarine descended with them.

"Hey, watch out!" Bud yelled. "We're going down into a canyon!"

He could see the volcanic stone ledges that had been worn smooth by pressure and tides of countless centuries.

Tom watched the instrument panel intently. "We're nearly halfway to the bottom!" he reported.

The drama of the situation plunged both boys into silence. They were doing something never achieved by human beings. Then Tom said tersely:

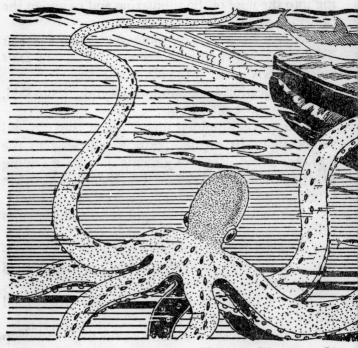

A maze of forty-foot-long tentacles

"Bud, we're at the bottom of the canyon."

"We left the squid behind," Bud reported. "I'll turn off the searchlight and see what happens."

Suddenly, as the boys looked out, they saw gigantic ribbons of intense light waving ahead of the bow.

"Switch on the light!" Tom cried.

When Bud did, the phosphorescence vanished. But in the strong beam was a terrifying sight. A maze of thick forty-foot-long tentacles was slithering toward them!

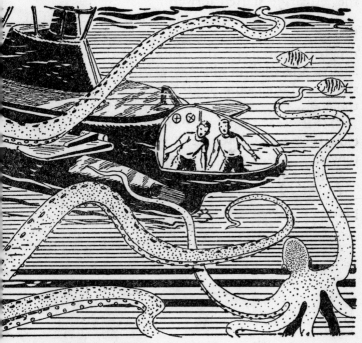

slithered toward the jetmarine

"It's a giant squid!" Tom yelled.

"As big as a submarine," Bud groaned. "Look at the size of its eye! Like a barrel top. We'd better shoot it!"

Tom mused for a second. "I hate to destroy this creature," he said. "I think we'll just get out of its way."

"You're a nice guy, Tom," Bud said fearfully, "but aren't you carrying your love of animals too far?"

Tom touched the controls at his finger tips and the jetmarine started forward.

"I think this will scare him," Tom said coolly. But he had not reckoned on a fight. With a vicious, lightninglike movement the squid lashed a tentacle against the nose of the *Sea Dart*. The submarine shuddered under the impact, throwing both boys to the floor.

"He'll break through!" Bud cried as the monster closed in around the bow with all its crushing tentacles.

"I'll shoot it!" Tom shouted.

He flung himself toward the instrument panel and pressed a button marked *oscillator gun*.

Nothing happened!

A look of despair came into Tom's eyes.

...

CHAPTER 17

A DANGEROUS TANGLE

WHEN THE oscillator ray gun failed to go off, Bud groaned. Tom pressed the firing button again. Still nothing happened.

By now the mammoth squid's writhing tentacles were tightening about the submarine's bow. Tom kept hoping that the horrible creature would not be able to crush the hull of the jetmarine. But there was still the danger of its damaging the controls!

Suddenly the young inventor cried out, "Bud, how stupid can I get? The gun's safety catch is on!"

With a quick flip he released the device and pressed the firing button again.

Vroooom!

The *Sea Dart* quivered from the recoil as the gun went off. The giant squid became a quivering mass, blown into a thousand bits of disorganized protoplasm.

"Jumping jets! What a show!" Bud shouted, as the remains of the creature slid away from the hull.

"Maybe that creature is nothing, though," Tom reflected, "compared to what we may see in outer space one of these days."

"Dreaming of that future rocket trip, eh?" Bud grinned. "Well, you can count me in on it, space monsters and all!"

Tom smiled as he touched a lever. The submarine's atomic power plant ejected a burst of energy which sent the jetmarine on its way upward and out of the canyon. A short time later Bud noticed signs of marine plant life.

"Shall we pick up some specimens of this seaweed?" he called.

Tom nodded and activated the intake nets to catch some of the sea growth. As he did this, Bud noticed a thick mass of seaweed ahead.

"Wow! That looks like a forest!" he shouted. "Do you think you can get through it, Tom?"

"We should be able to easily," the skipper replied. "I'll give her a little extra juice."

The *Sea Dart* penetrated deep into the dense mass. At first the submarine cut through the barrier cleanly, but all at once it stopped dead.

"Tom, what happened?" Bud shouted as he pitched forward.

The power plant continued to operate but the jetmarine failed to move an inch.

"We're not getting propulsion," Tom shouted.

Both boys hurried to the stern, where Tom removed the metal housing from the jet mechanism. A look of bewilderment came over his face.

"No wonder, Bud!" he exclaimed. "We're not getting any water in the steam chambers! The intake ports are clogged with seaweed. Our baffle screens weren't fine enough to keep the stuff out."

"Boy, we're really in a fix," Bud said slowly.

"We'll be in a worse one if we don't hurry!" Tom shouted as he wheeled about. "Look at that heat gauge. The steam chambers will blow up if we don't shut off the pile!"

Tom dashed to the control room and flipped a lever which stopped the atomic reaction.

Bud followed him, his face pale with anxiety. "How are we going to clear out those jammed intake ports so we can move the *Sea Dart*, Tom?"

"I'm not sure," Tom replied slowly.

"You're not stumped, are you?" Bud asked anxiously.

"Let me think about it for a while," Tom replied.

Together, the boys went forward to examine the intake ports. They found them matted shut by masses of sodden green plant life.

Tom ran his fingers through his hair. "You see, Bud, what an inventor's up against? Our atomic plant is powerful enough to propel us through this mass, but if we lack one ingredient—sea water—the jets won't work."

Tom pondered in silence for several minutes. Then he snapped his fingers and said:

"There are two possibilities for our escape, Bud."

"Name them, professor," Bud replied grimly.

"First, we could blow our ballast tanks and try to float up through the mass of weeds. But we'd have to use most of our oxygen to do it."

"It would be mighty risky," Bud reasoned.

"Right. Which leads to another proposition. I have an idea there's enough seepage through the ports to fill our water chambers after a while. We could wait for this to happen, then start the pile, and give her one big blast of propulsion."

Bud grinned. "If there's not too much gook above us, we might crash through."

"Exactly."

"I have an idea too," Bud said. "If nothing else works, we could put on our escape suits and cut through the weeds until we reach the top."

"Fair enough," Tom replied. "But don't forget, we'll be awfully lonesome bobbing on the surface of the sea so many miles from shore. And what if Dansitt's sub should spot us before a friendly vessel might?"

"I guess you're right, Tom," Bud agreed, making a wry face. "We'll have to wait until enough sea water seeps into our tanks."

Tom beckoned Bud to follow him and went forward. Near the nose of the jetmarine, Tom got down on all fours and wriggled through a narrow opening which led to the starboard intake port.

"Water is trickling through all right," Tom shouted. "We shouldn't have to wait much longer than an hour for the tanks to fill."

To while away the time, Bud took out a deck of

cards and did a few tricks. But Tom, restless, watched anxiously as the sea water gradually filled the steam chambers. Finally, after several inspections, he shouted:

"Okay, Bud, we're set to go."

The young inventor double-checked the tanks, seated himself before the control-room panel, and cried to Bud, "Use your headrest, pal. This will be a rapid acceleration."

"Like an underseas rocket, eh?"

Tom flipped the lever and the atomic pile roared into operation. With a tremendous hissing sound the salt water generated into steam. The turbine blades spun and shot sea water out of the stern of the submarine. With a sudden lurch the submarine leaped forward.

"Tom, we made it!" Bud shouted as the *Sea Dart* cleared the seaweed and rose higher into the dense green sea.

"Now I think it's safe to shoot some air into our ballast tanks," Tom said.

"Okay, skipper."

In a few seconds the submarine, buoyed by the charge of air, rushed toward the surface. When it broke through the waves, Bud threw open the hatch.

"Boy, that blue sky looks good to me!" he exclaimed.

"No time for daydreaming," Tom replied. "If we don't hurry, the pirates will reach Spaniel Island ahead of us. We've got to get these ports cleared pronto."

Tom opened a locker and hauled out two pairs of goggles and diving fins. Quickly the boys got into their swimming trunks, pulled the fins over their feet, adjusted the goggles, and dived in. Both were excellent underwater swimmers and had the weeds removed from the intake ports within ten minutes.

As soon as they had rested a bit, Tom set his atomic pile in action again and submerged to periscope depth, and once more headed for Spaniel Island.

Within an hour darkness began to settle over the sea. Bud was amusing himself by tuning in to various radio programs and signals being received by their powerful equipment.

"Keep your ears open for a message from home, will you, Bud?" Tom asked. "Don't forget it will be scrambled, but we can run it through our code machine."

During the next half-hour, Bud picked up several scrambled messages, but after feeding them to the machine, he realized that they were not in the Swifts' code.

"Let's switch around, Tom," Bud said. "I'm getting tired of being a listening post."

"Okay."

Bud took the wheel, and Tom relieved him at the radio receiver. As Bud was talking about his favorite baseball team's league standing, Tom suddenly held up his hand for silence.

"There's a very faint scrambled signal coming over," he said. "Listen!"

Bud cut the motors to low speed to reduce the vibration and Tom fed the message into his decoding machine. At first the two boys could not make it out. The sounds came through very feebly, as if they were being whispered.

"Is the intensifier on full?" Tom asked.

Bud checked it. "No, I can give her more juice."

Now the message came from the unscrambler a little louder.

"Jumping jets!" Bud cried. "It sounds like Uncle Ned's voice."

"You're right!"

As Tom and Bud listened in icy terror the message was repeated. Faintly Ned Newton was saying:

"Pirates plan to capture Foster yacht. Warn them at once!"

"The Foster yacht!" Bud exclaimed. "Your dad's in danger!"

CHAPTER 18

KIDNAPED!

THE MESSAGE from Ned Newton continued, growing weaker each second.

" 'Dogs' plan to kidnap—" The rest was lost.

The news stunned Bud and Tom. Did the pirates plan to kidnap Mr. Swift and others aboard the *Primrose?* The boys realized they must act quickly! Before they had a chance to start formulating a plan, the radio message was audible again, but much feebler.

"Three hours out of Miami," came Ned Newton's voice. He repeated this, then no more was heard from the pirates' prisoner.

"If only we dared radio Uncle Ned now," Bud groaned. "He could give us more details about the pirates' plans."

Tom, for a moment, was tempted to do just this and at least let Ned Newton know he and Bud were nearby and had picked up the warning message. But

he quickly put aside the idea and determined to ob-
serve his uncle's original caution against contacting
him. No use antagonizing the pirates into taking
vengeful action against their prisoner.

As if reading Tom's conflicting thoughts, Bud laid
a hand on his friend's shoulder. "We'll stop that
gang somehow!"

Tom nodded as he studied the large chart on the
wall. "Yes, Bud, we must try to get to the *Primrose*
first!"

Bud pointed to a certain area on the map. "Three
hours out of Miami toward Spaniel Island would
put the Foster yacht right about here, wouldn't it?"
he asked.

Tom looked skeptical. "Actually we have no idea
what direction they took. Dad may have wanted to
approach the island from the far side and taken a
northerly or southerly route to reach it. But let's try
the direct route first."

As he spoke, the jetmarine surfaced, and Tom increased her speed.

"This baby really rips along on the surface!" Bud
commented as he watched the log indicator.

Within an hour the boys were in the general area
where the *Primrose* might be expected to be sailing. Now, with Bud at the wheel and Tom at the
radarscope, the boys crisscrossed the area, being
careful to take note of every craft within reach of
the radar beams.

A coastwise freighter, several commercial fishing
boats, and a small cruiser hove into sight. Each was

examined minutely through the submarine's instruments before the boys decided that none was the *Primrose*.

As the minutes slowly passed, Tom's face took on a worried expression. "I don't like to say this, Bud, but I'm afraid the pirates reached the *Primrose* ahead of us."

"In that case," said Bud, "they will be sailing her toward Spaniel Island. Let's go!"

"That's sound reasoning," Tom agreed. "We'll try it."

He submerged to periscope depth in order to avoid detection by the pirates and reduced speed in order not to overlook a single craft that might come into view on their screen. Several coastwise ships of sizable tonnage passed above, but the boys did not sight the yacht.

"We're just about to the end of the possible distance the *Primrose* could have made in this length of time," Tom said finally. "Maybe we should try another direction."

Bud glanced anxiously at the radarscope. Tom was about to turn the wheel of the jetmarine when his friend shouted:

"Look at the screen! This may be it, Tom!"

"Whatever the ship is, she's not making any headway," Tom remarked. "We'd better investigate."

"Ten to one it's the *Primrose!*" Bud exclaimed.

"Prepare to surface!" Tom ordered.

In a few moments the *Sea Dart* broke into the evening darkness. Tom and Bud clambered through the escape hatch. Stars were twinkling and the sky was streaked with thin, wispy clouds. The moon provided enough light so that the boys could make out a yacht listing badly to port.

"There's not a light aboard!" Bud exclaimed. "That's strange!"

Tom trained his glasses on the craft. "The *Primrose!* And the decks are empty." Then he cupped his hands and cried out:

"Hello. Hello, *Primrose!*"

There was no reply.

Fear clutched the hearts of the two boys. The *Primrose* lay stricken and deserted before them. The pirates had already struck!

Tom, the first to regain his composure, said, "We'll board her and see if we can find out what happened."

As he started below, intending to guide the jet-marine alongside the other vessel, there came the whine of bullets skimming the waves.

"Duck!" Tom shouted.

Bud moved quickly behind the steel wall of the escape hatch as white spray was kicked up in the sea about him.

Tom peered out cautiously. "Somebody's aboard —probably the pirates!"

Another burst bounced off the Tomasite covering of the conning tower.

It suddenly occurred to Tom that it might be the *Primrose's* crew firing, having mistaken the *Sea Dart* for the enemy.

"I'll find out in a second," he determined.

He stripped off his white skivvy shirt and waved it aloft. The submarine and the yacht had drifted closer together and Tom knew his cries could be heard on the deck of the *Primrose.*

"Don't shoot!" he shouted. "We're friends. We've come to help you."

The firing ceased. A moment later the dim shape of a head appeared over the rail.

"Who are you? What do you want?" a man called suspiciously.

"We're Tom Swift and Bud Barclay," the young skipper shouted.

At the mention of these names several more heads appeared above the rail.

"All right," came the same voice again. "We'll drop a boat to get you!"

"Never mind," Tom said. "I can come aboard."

He disappeared down the hatch and soon maneuvered the jetmarine alongside the *Primrose.* When the craft had been lashed, Tom and Bud climbed a Jacob's ladder to the yacht deck. A tall, slender man in uniform greeted them.

"I'm George White, skipper of the *Primrose,*" he said, as the rest of the crew stood by.

Tom acknowledged the introduction. Then he scanned the faces about him in the gloom.

"Where are my father and Mr. Foster?" Tom asked anxiously.

The skipper hesitated.

"What happened?" Bud insisted.

Captain White cleared his throat. "They were kidnaped," he said finally, his voice shaky.

"By the pirates?" Tom questioned.

"Yes," Captain White answered.

"You were right, Tom," Bud said, "they beat us to it."

"We thought you were part of the gang coming back," the skipper explained. "That's why we fired on you. We were sure that it was another trick."

"How did they attack you?" Bud asked, knowing that with a distorter aboard, the blackout ray would not work.

"They didn't use a plane or a sub," Captain White answered. "That's why we fell into their trap."

He said that the pirates had approached the *Primrose* in a small motor launch. Their leader had called up to the deck of the yacht, saying that they had been lost in a squall, were nearly out of fuel, and asked for transportation to the nearest port.

"Like fools we invited them on board," Captain White said, shaking his head sadly. "Then they knocked us out and tied us up. We just got loose an hour ago. We found the yacht's sea cocks open and the radio and motors disabled. We still can't get them started."

"But what happened to my father and Mr. Foster?" Tom asked impatiently. "Where did the pirates take them?"

A seaman stepped forward. "I overheard one of those kidnapers say that your father and Mr. Foster would be taken to the North Woods."

"The North Woods?" Bud echoed.

The seaman paused as if he was weighing the advisability of telling any more bad news.

"Yes, go on," Tom urged.

The man looked at the deck as he said, "The pirates said they're going to hold them until—until two people named Dansitt and Chilcote accomplish certain work and rid the Caribbean of Tom Swift Jr!"

CHAPTER 19

HOT PURSUIT

"GET ME out of the Caribbean?" Tom exclaimed. "Never!"

"You're right, pal." Bud said grimly. "But if your dad is held prisoner in the North Woods—"

"That's what I heard," the sailor insisted.

Tom looked at Bud. "I don't believe he is. My guess is that it's a false lead to head us off. I think Dad and Mr. Foster are on Spaniel Island along with Uncle Ned. And the sooner we get there the better."

Tom could see from the look in his friend's eyes that Bud did not share this opinion entirely. He added:

"We won't take any chances, though. I'll notify the authorities about the North Woods clue."

Tom hurried down the Jacob's ladder and went through the hatch of the *Sea Dart*. Using the scrambled speech device, he radioed to the Enterprises plant. After a long wait Hanson came on, having been summoned from home.

Tom broke the news of the kidnaping of his father and Mr. Foster. He asked Hanson to relay it as kindly as possible to Mrs. Swift and Sandy.

"I'm shocked to hear this news, Tom, Your family has never been in such serious trouble. Dansitt and the others really knew the way to hit you where it hurts the most—your father."

Tom agreed. Then he told Hanson about the clue which the pirates had dropped concerning a hideout in the North Woods.

"We won't leave a stone unturned," Hanson promised. "I'll notify the police to start a search there. In the meantime, Sterling and I will start at dawn and fly the *Sky Queen* over the area to see if we can pick up any information."

Before signing off, Tom asked if the prisoner in the Shopton jail had confessed yet.

"No," Hanson replied. "Not a word out of him."

Tom turned off the set and hurried up to the deck. Two seamen who were topside the *Primrose* told him that Bud had gone below with the captain to help repair the machinery the pirates had damaged. Tom climbed aboard and went down the iron stairs into the engine room to assist them.

"Those devils disconnected wires somewhere," Bud said. "And we can't find them."

Tom systematically examined the electrical system. Fifteen minutes later he whistled to Bud.

"Over this way. I've found it—two disconnected cables behind the meter board."

After the damage had been repaired and Tom had helped restore the radio and wireless service, he returned to the deck to speak to Captain White.

"Tom," the officer said, "there's another clue from the pirates you might like to have. Something to do with a girl named Jane Pitt. One of them laughed and whispered to another pirate, 'I'll certainly be glad to see her.' "

Bud's eyes widened. "Maybe they're going into the kidnaping business on a big scale."

"I don't think it's kidnaping this time," Tom said. "My hunch is Jane Pitt is the name of a ship that's going to be the pirate's next victim." He turned to Captain White. "Have you a ship registry on board?"

The captain said he did and hurried to the cabin. Tom followed. Quickly running down the list of ships, his finger came to the name *Jane Pitt*. She was of Panamanian registry and plied the sea lanes between the Caribbean and eastern Atlantic ports. Even the sea lane she traveled was given.

"If we can locate the *Jane Pitt* before the pirates attack—" Tom said excitedly.

"You mean face those pirates almost single-handed!" Bud cried.

"There's no other way," Tom declared. "And not a minute to lose, Bud. Come on!"

Captain White tried his utmost to dissuade the boys from going.

"You'll be so outnumbered," he insisted, "those pirates won't have much trouble getting you out of the Caribbean—as they've threatened."

"I'll take that chance," Tom replied. "The distorter is the only way to stop them. This is my big opportunity to follow the pirates to their hide-out and capture them."

The others did not argue longer. The boys said good-by and returned to the jetmarine. Once the lines were cast off, Tom headed toward the shipping lane in which the *Jane Pitt* would be traveling. While Bud took over the controls, Tom again sent a scrambled message to Shopton, asking Hanson to find out about the ship's location from the company which owned it.

"I'll do it at once," Hanson promised. "Too bad a warning to the *Jane Pitt* wouldn't do any good. That blackout ray is a devilish device."

"Which I hope to ruin," Tom said.

Twenty minutes later he had the data he wanted from Hanson. The shipping company had supplied longitude and latitude at which the freighter was due within the next half-hour.

"What luck!" Bud cried. "We're close enough to the *Jane Pitt* to give her a wolf whistle."

Tom was staring hard at the sonarscope. A bright spot of light had appeared.

"It's not a freighter, I'm sure," Tom said slowly.

"The pirate sub?" Bud asked. "I hope that they won't try to ram us!"

"Don't let them," Tom replied. "It could be a Navy sub. We'll soon know."

"Shall we tail it?" Bud asked.

In answer, Tom trimmed the ballast tanks, sending the jetmarine lower into the sea. Then both boys kept eyes alerted on the echo equipment.

"The other craft has surfaced and is making no headway," Bud reported. "Isn't it just about time for the *Jane Pitt* to show up?"

The question had no sooner been asked when the presence of a vessel could be detected. Bud charted its position. "She's off to our starboard about two miles," he said.

Tom guided the *Sea Dart* in a wide sweep, and submerging another thirty feet, headed toward the oncoming freighter.

"We'll let her pass right over us," he said. "Then we'll surface and cover her from behind. We'll pick up the pirate plane with the night radar on the bridge. The minute it starts its run, we'll short-circuit his focusing device with the distorter."

"I'm with you, jet boy," Bud replied tersely.

In a few minutes the sonarscope indicated that the freighter was passing directly over the jetmarine.

"You can feel her engines pounding," Tom said excitedly, and immediately angled the submarine sharply toward the surface. He swung her about in pursuit of the freighter, quickly closing the distance and hovering only two hundred yards astern. Then he rose to periscope depth and Bud turned on the radar.

His face muscles grew taut as he watched the screen. Suddenly he shouted:

"A plane! It's on the screen, Tom! Bearing 290 degrees from us, about a mile on our portside."

Tensely the two waited, their eyes glued on the screen to follow the plane's approach. The next moment it dived for a blackout attack on the *Jane Pitt!*

"*Now!*" Tom cried and pressed the key of his distorter!

CHAPTER 20

BOOMERANG TACTICS

THE MOMENT the pirate plane passed, Tom surfaced and gunned the jetmarine toward the *Jane Pitt*. Running the submarine close along the portside, he called out through his powered megaphone:

"Ahoy, there!"

No answer. Tom's heart sank. Could his distorter have failed to short-circuit the assault? But a moment later his fear was dispelled when a booming voice answered:

"This is Captain Jones. What can we do for you?"

"Are you all right?" Tom cried.

"Yes. Why not?"

Tom identified himself and quickly told the skipper what he suspected. The captain, completely flabbergasted by the news that his ship had just escaped attack by pirates, answered:

"We thought the pilot was in trouble and flying lower than he realized."

"I think you're going to be boarded," Tom continued, keeping the jetmarine a safe distance from the rolling ship. "Any minute now you can—"

He broke off abruptly. The pirates' jet was whistling in from the portside!

"Here he comes again!" Tom called to Bud, and instantly aimed his distorter in the direction of the sound.

As the plane zoomed in, Tom swung the distorter sharply upward at the low-flying plane. There was a cry from the *Jane Pitt* and sweat poured from the young inventor's forehead when he realized that the distorter might not have been a hundred per cent effective during this unexpected follow-up attack. He himself might lose the *Sea Dart* to the pirates—to say nothing of being captured!

Then, to his intense relief, the captain called down, "You still there?"

"Yes. We must work fast, though," Tom replied. "If I've figured this thing right, you'll be boarded by pirates from a submarine."

"We took several Marines aboard to help us fight in case of an attack," Captain Jones told him. "They'll take care of any pirates!"

Quickly Tom explained that the raiders were probably under the leadership of a very clever scientist and it was possible that the usual methods of armed defense might not be effective against them.

"What can we do, then, Mr. Swift?" the officer asked, his tone betraying a note of despair.

"I'll keep my distorter working," Tom offered,

"and watch the pirate sub for any funny business. How about having your men pretend to be unconscious? Then, after the pirates fan out on your ship, tackle them one by one."

"We'll do it!" Captain Jones said.

"Here comes the plane again!" Tom cried. "The pilot must know his ray hasn't worked yet."

"He'll think so this time!" Captain Jones assured Tom, and barked orders to his men and the Marines in line with Tom's suggestion.

Meanwhile, Tom asked Bud to move the *Sea Dart* beyond the stern of the ship, so they might keep a closer watch on the enemy's procedure. As the plane swooped in again, this time very low, the engines of the freighter quivered, then stopped. Lights went out. Marines and crewmen became silent. In fact, the silence was so prolonged that Bud murmured anxiously:

"Maybe the blackout worked this time."

Tom, too, was tense, wondering what was happening aboard the freighter. From the starboard the jetmarine's radar picked up the pirate submarine moving in for the kill.

"Here they come!" Tom said as a brilliant searchlight suddenly focused on the center of the long freighter. The *Sea Dart* was safely outside the circle of white light.

In the rear of the beams Tom could see several dim figures on the deck of a giant submarine. One of the men began to issue orders.

"Gilson! Croat! Board her!"

The two pirates, one carrying a heavy coiled rope, executed a daring leap from the deck to the swinging rope ladder on the portside and started their climb up the side. Apparently they were so confident about the power of the blackout weapon that they did not even unfasten their gun-holster flaps.

Tom leaped down the hatch, a plan in mind to see what was about to happen on deck. Quickly he ran the extension of the periscope to its full height, which was many feet beyond that which is usually used. Next, he adjusted the television cameras to pick up what was on the sights and threw the picture on the screen. It was clear and well defined.

"Look!" he called excitedly to Bud as he stepped up the sound receivers.

The first pirate had just reached the deck and called down to his slower accomplice, "These guys are out cold!"

He reached down and assisted the other man aboard. Then they headed for the hatchway that led to the engine room. Gilson went first, stepping onto the grilled iron platform that supported the ladder.

Gilson, reaching forward to clutch the rail, suddenly was stunned by a fierce blow on the back of his skull. He pitched headlong, down the steel steps.

Croat, following close behind, was clubbed simultaneously by a burly seaman who a moment before had appeared to be an unconscious man lying face down on the grill.

Two oilers dashed up from below, dragging the men out on deck. They tied up the unconscious pirates and hid them behind a locker.

As the *Jane Pitt* swayed in the roughening sea, the pirate skipper called out, "Croat, where's that second ladder? Get it over the side! And shake a leg, man, before the crew wakes up!"

One of the *Jane Pitt* deck hands, keeping his head out of sight, quickly lowered the requested ladder.

"Get going, the rest of you!" the pirate commander shouted. "You lazy, low-down fools, do you want to be caught?"

Two at a time the men started to scramble up the ladders. As the first pirate swung his leg over the gunwale, Tom and Bud could see a black-sleeved arm extended to assist him.

"Okay, Croat," the fellow said. "I guess—"

The hand tightened like a steel clamp on his throat and he was dragged quietly out of sight. The first man up the other ladder got the same treatment.

"Say, there goes the skipper himself!" Tom called out as the man joined the last three pirates who were now scampering up the ropes.

Before they got to the top, Tom said excitedly to Bud:

"Take over here, will you? Keep this movie camera going."

"You got a movie of this?" Bud asked incredulously. "Wow! What evidence! Where are you going?" he asked as Tom started away.

"To capture that sub and its captain."

"What!"

"If you'll maneuver the jetmarine alongside, I'll jump to their deck."

"That's pretty risky."

"I realize that," Tom replied. "But if I can knock out the pirate in the control room before he suspects what has happened on the *Jane Pitt,* he can't get away."

"This sounds like the days of Captain Kidd!" Bud said. "Okay, I'll throttle down to six knots as I go

With a tremendous leap Tom cleared the rails

past, then circle around and come back for you in ten minutes."

Bud kept a keen eye on the enemy craft as the jetmarine slid closer and closer to it.

Tom went on deck and waited tensely. A huge wave slapped the conning tower and nearly swung the prow of the *Sea Dart* against the stern of the pirate submarine, but Bud deftly maneuvered out of the way in time.

Then the moment came. The submarines were only six feet apart. With a tremendous leap Tom cleared the railing of the pirate submarine. The jet-marine vanished in the darkness.

Cautiously Tom moved forward toward the conning tower. A dim light shone from the open hatch. Tom had almost reached the hatchway when he was startled by the appearance of a man's head in the light.

Sidney Dansitt! Tom had assumed that he was the pilot of the blackout plane!

For a second Dansitt glared at Tom in complete astonishment. Then the look was followed instantly by one of fierce hatred. As Tom sprang toward him, the young pirate called down the hatch:

"Get under way fast! Submerge!"

Before Tom could reach the tower, Dansitt had slammed down the cover and locked it.

Tom was trapped on the submerging deck!

CHAPTER 21

TOM IS TRAPPED

AS THE SEA WATER swirled about Tom's feet, he clutched the guardrail of the pirate submarine. He did not dare dive overboard. The churning water might suck him into the propeller blades.

Then another awful truth struck him. He was already a good distance from the *Jane Pitt*. Even if he survived a jump into the sea, Bud would not know this. He would assume that Tom was a prisoner on board and not look for him in the water.

Tom suddenly realized that Dansitt had stopped submerging. What was the reason? Was it because he wanted to torture Tom before leaving him to an almost certain death? Dansitt had an advantage now which he had never achieved in their former encounters.

Staring ahead helplessly, Tom's eyes caught an insigne on the conning tower. A devilfish!

"An appropriate name for a devil's sub!" Tom muttered.

He realized that, although the *Devilfish* was not an atomic-powered submarine, it was built for war and seemed to be as fast as anything possessed by the navies of the world at the moment. Was this sharp-nosed craft an invention of Chilcote's?

The lights on the *Jane Pitt* grew dim in the distance. The jetmarine was out of sight. Still Dansitt did not submerge. Tom wondered why.

Suddenly he knew. As the submarine made a wide sweep and headed back in the direction from which it had come, the *Sea Dart* loomed up in the distance. The *Devilfish* steered straight toward the smaller submarine. It could ram the jetmarine with little damage to itself!

"Bud! Bud! Look out!" Tom cried, knowing full well his partner could not hear the anguished plea.

But the *Sea Dart* did not move off its course. Tom kept his eyes glued on the hull of his prized invention as Dansitt sped closer and closer to it. Would it be a grave for his best friend at the bottom of the sea?

Tom could not bear to look as the distance closed between the two craft. But just as there should have been a crash, he heard a swishing noise. The jetmarine had passed them! It had swerved and cleared the enemy craft by only a few feet!

Now Tom realized Bud's strategy. He had waited until the last split second to maneuver the two-man submarine out of the way! A moment later Tom was nearly thrown into the water by an abrupt turn of the pirate craft, indicating the anger of Dansitt. But by the time the *Devilfish* was poised for another strike, the jetmarine had submerged. Even its periscope was not visible.

Tom's elation was short-lived as Dansitt also began to submerge. The waves tore at Tom's ankles, then his knees.

"I must take a chance and jump!" Tom decided.

He climbed on the rail, poised for a second, then gave a tremendous outward leap, landing in the water a safe distance beyond the suction of the *Devilfish*. As it continued its dive, he swam underwater with every ounce of strength at his command.

Rising to the surface, he found it turbulent with foamy whitecaps. Salt water filled Tom's eyes, nose, and mouth as he swam down into the trough of one wave and up the side of another. He waved frantically toward the *Jane Pitt* and an empty feeling seized him as the freighter continued to move in the opposite direction.

Never before had Tom felt so utterly vanquished. He was in the middle of the Caribbean without even a life preserver or a piece of driftwood on which to hold. Just how long his strength would last was a matter of conjecture. Tom knew it could not be long.

Growing weaker by the minute, he turned over and floated aimlessly. One wave slapped over his head, then another. Tom swallowed some of the sea water. His head began to whirl and his lungs ached.

And where was Bud? Had the *Devilfish* found the jetmarine and sunk it?

Suddenly his feet touched a hard surface. "A shark!" was Tom's first thought.

Then, as if by a miracle, he found himself, flat on his back, on the deck of a surfacing submarine.

"Has Dansitt come back to torment me?" the young inventor asked himself, knowing that he was without strength to fight back. Coughing out salt water and trying to suck fresh air into his lungs, Tom turned his head weakly and saw the hatch fly open.

"Bud, Bud—!" he uttered and sank back exhausted as his friend sprang forward to assist him.

He carried Tom to his bunk, swathed him in heavy blankets, and brought him a hot drink. A few minutes later Tom fell into a deep sleep. Awaking, he asked:

"How long have I been out?"

"Not long, you old sea dog." Bud grinned. "About a half-hour, I'd say. I sure had an awful time finding you."

Tom smiled back. "How did you do it?"

Bud told how he had shaken off the enemy submarine, then through the periscope had seen Tom floundering in the water.

"I figured the easiest way to pick you up was topside," Bud explained.

"Well, thanks, pal, for robbing some shark of a free dinner," Tom said. "You did a wonderful job."

Bud replied, grinning, "Well, when it comes to fish dinners, boy, I guess I'm not a bad navigator at that."

"Bud, we can't stay here," Tom said. "Even though I feel like a beat-up porpoise, we have work to do and quickly."

"Take it easy, chum."

"No," Tom replied. "We must get going right away."

"Where?"

"Let's submerge and contact the *Jane Pitt*. I want to question those pirates who were captured."

In spite of Bud's protests, Tom insisted on continuing their mission. While he rested for a few minutes, Bud tried to contact the ship. Failing, he surfaced the jetmarine and headed through the dim light of dawn in the direction which the freighter had taken.

Applying full speed, the craft skimmed over the surface of the sea. Soon it was alongside the *Jane Pitt* and Tom called to Captain Jones that he wanted to come aboard.

"I'd like to question your prisoners, Captain," he said. "They may know something about my father and Mr. Foster who were kidnaped."

Since it was impractical in the rough water to bring the submarine close enough for a jump to the rope ladder, the officer ordered a lifeboat swung out on a davit over the deck of the submarine. Tom climbed into it and was hoisted aboard.

The captain led him below to a half-empty hold

where the prisoners were securely chained. Sullen and ugly, they glowered as Tom approached and introduced himself.

"What do you know about my father, Mr. Swift?" he asked sternly. "Where is he?"

When they did not answer, Tom looked into the face of each pirate, hoping to find some sign which might betray one of them as being more humane than the others. He studied the face of a thin, wiry man, who had a grizzly stubble and shifty eyes.

Tom grasped the prisoner's shirt front in his right fist and pulled him close. "What do you know about my father and Mr. Foster?" he demanded.

When the pirate did not reply, Tom shook him. At the same time the captain spoke up.

"These men ought to be tied hand and foot and thrown overboard!"

As Tom nodded agreement, the thin man quavered. "No, no, don't do that!" he pleaded. "I'll tell you what you want to know."

Before he had a chance to, another of the prisoners hurled himself in front of the speaker. "Shut up!" he snarled.

Intimidated, the grizzled sailor said no more, but his companion went on gruffly, "You think you're smart with your distorter, Tom Swift. Yes, the boss found out about it but he's got somethin' up his sleeve that's more powerful than his pulsator."

"Where is he heading—Spaniel Island?" Tom asked sharply.

The pirate's eyes widened momentarily, and

though he did not answer, Tom felt sure that his query had struck home.

Thanking the captain, he hurried from the hold and was hoisted back to the *Sea Dart*. Quickly he told Bud of the new threat, then said:

"No matter what weapon Chilcote may have, we're going full speed ahead to Spaniel Island!"

CHAPTER 22

PERILOUS WATERS

THE YOUNG SUBMARINERS kept careful watch for the *Devilfish* as they made their way toward Spaniel Island.

"If that baby is headed for the same place we are, she sure has terrific speed. We should have sighted her by now," Bud said.

Tom surfaced the jetmarine twice in order to make better time, but when merchant ships hove into view, he dived again to avoid answering any queries which their radiomen might send out.

Bud, meanwhile, had kept his eyes on the radar and sonarscopes. Presently the sonarscope picked up a submarine.

"This may be the *Devilfish*," Bud cried eagerly.

When the radar failed to pick up anything above the surface of the sea the boys were sure they had found Dansitt's craft.

As the *Sea Dart* gained on the submarine, Tom

contacted Shopton by radio. He learned that Sterling and Hanson had gone to the North Woods in the *Sky Queen* to assist the police in their search for Mr. Swift and Mr. Foster, but so far had discovered nothing.

"That convinces me all the more they're at Spaniel Island," Tom said.

Drawing closer to the enemy submarine, Bud remarked, "Lucky they can't detect us! That invention of yours sure is a honey, Tom. Are you going to follow the *Devilfish* right into Dog's Collar Channel?" he asked.

"No, I'll wait until I think it's safe."

Tom studied his chart, then blew the ballast tank until the periscope nicked the top of the green waves. He turned the handle and swept the horizon.

"There she is to port!" he said excitedly. "Spaniel Island! And Dansitt is heading directly for the channel."

"Now what do we do?" Bud inquired.

"We'll stand by and see what develops. I'm sure the pirates have these waters fortified against such visitors as ourselves."

He stood aside while Bud glued his eyes to the periscope.

"There doesn't seem to be a thing on the island, Tom," Bud remarked. "Oh, yes, I see something now. It looks like a fisherman's hut among those leaning trees."

"The pirates' hide-out must be underground," Tom said.

"Or under water," Bud conjectured.

"We'll soon find out," Tom said.

As he cut the motors, the periscope picked up an unusual sight. The *Devilfish* had surfaced four hundred yards ahead and was zigzagging cautiously toward Dog's Collar Channel.

"Oh, oh," Bud said, turning from the eyepiece. "The place is mined!"

"I thought so," Tom remarked. "Well, let's see what Dansitt does now."

Tom flipped the television connection to the periscope, and he and Bud had a front-row seat in the drama unfolding before them. The *Devilfish* cut left and right and straight ahead again, threading her way through what the boys believed was a mine field.

"Pretty clever," Bud remarked. "I wish we had their chart."

"We don't need a road map," Tom remarked, smiling at his partner. "I'll take her down and we can look around. If it's not too dangerous, we'll try to negotiate the mines ourselves."

"The *Devilfish* is submerging again!" Bud cried.

Dansitt's craft disappeared when it was not more than thirty yards from the shore of Spaniel Island.

"That sub's berth is under water for sure!" Bud said. "Now what will we do, genius boy?"

Tom failed to answer immediately. He was switching on the periscope's telescopic lens. Peering at the screen he pointed to the right side of the narrow entrance.

"Look!" he cried. "There's part of a wooden barrel drifting with the current into the channel!"

"What are we going to do—get into the barrel?" Bud asked, keeping a straight face.

Tom grinned. "That barrel gave me an idea!"

"What doesn't give you an idea?" Bud laughed.

"Seriously," Tom continued, "we're going to hug the shore and come around that bend just the way the barrel did. Our real hazard will be the rapid current."

"But how about the mines?" Bud asked. "We'll be blown to smithereens!"

"We'll have to be sure we don't contact them," Tom replied calmly. "We'll steer past them."

"Why don't we just blow up the mines and go in?" Bud asked. "Dansitt will think we struck one of them and won't worry about us."

"He might also think we blew them up intentionally," Tom countered, "and we'd be depth-charged to a fare-thee-well."

"Maybe you're right." Bud groaned.

"And besides," Tom added, "we have no way of exploding those mines, anyway."

"What's the matter with the ray gun?" Bud asked quickly.

Tom shook his head. "Our gun wouldn't have any effect on them," he replied. "They're probably contact mines and we'd have to hit them with some kind of a projectile."

"And we have no projectiles," Bud said meekly.

"Exactly," Tom replied quietly. "And what's

more, I think we'd better turn on our jet and swing around to the shore now while they're busy inside there with the *Devilfish*."

With a single motion Tom swung the rudder and cut in the sub's full power. The *Sea Dart* streaked like a scared barracuda toward the rock-ledged shore. The wide arc ended as Tom reduced speed about a hundred feet from the channel mouth.

Bringing the submarine flush against the almost vertical natural rock walls of the island, he gunned it gently until he felt the deep currents take hold of the craft. Then, turning off the power, he looked into the periscope and saw that they were moving slowly past the shore line.

"Now we go to the bottom!" the inventor announced, twisting the valves to take on full ballast. The submarine lowered gradually into the fast-moving water.

"Run into the nose and keep reporting what you see until we come to the corner," Tom called to Bud. "And when you see the end of the rock wall notify me fast. Our lives will depend on it!"

Bud dashed forward and took up his position in the transparent bow.

As the jetmarine neared the deadly entrance, Bud called out, "Are you sure you want to go through with this, Tom? We have enough evidence that this is the pirates' hide-out. We never can capture those men alone. What say we leave and send for help?"

"We've got to continue," Tom replied as the submarine gained momentum. "According to the first message we got from Uncle Ned, this may be his last day here. And if my father and Mr. Foster are on the island, they may be in just as dangerous a situation. I can't let them down, Bud."

"Don't pay any more attention to me," said Bud. "I was only making small talk!"

Suddenly his eye caught sight of mounds of fresh debris lying along the bottom.

"Tom!" Bud called. "They've recently blasted and dredged this channel!" He was about to tell Tom why he knew this when the submarine reached the entrance. "Hard right!" he cried. "We're at the corner!"

The sharp current fairly pulled the bow of the *Sea Dart* around the turn. As the craft straightened into her 90° thrust into the channel, Tom gave her quarter speed for a moment and steered the submarine even harder against the channel bank. In here, too, the rock walls went straight down.

"I see a mine!" Bud cried.

The words sent a chill down Tom's spine.

"Where is it?" he called.

"About ten feet to the left of our bow!" Bud called back.

Tom held the rudder fast. The right side of the submarine hull scraped slightly on the rock as the current sucked it farther and farther into the lair of the pirates.

"We missed it—by inches!" Bud murmured thankfully.

He took a deep breath and continued staring through the nose of the bow. Dead ahead, about fif-

"I see a mine," Bud cried

teen feet, there loomed the ominous black spherical shape of another mine.

"Come left—hard!" Bud called in terror.

Tom gunned the jet and swung the rudder. Bud could see the black horns of the deadly mine as the bow eased past it.

Tom allowed the craft to drift its length before he headed it back to the right bank. His heart was pounding as he felt the submarine gently touch the rock again.

"Nothing ahead now," Bud called. "We must be almost in there!"

"Don't be too sure," Tom warned him.

He had hardly finished saying this when Bud shouted, "Tom, a submarine net! It's right in front of us."

Tom halted the jetmarine and went forward to take a look himself. A heavy cable made of thick wire barred his passage up the channel.

"They probably slipped this into place after the *Devilfish* went in," Bud said.

"Exactly," Tom said. "But it won't stop us. Get me the undersea cutting equipment while I put on a Fat Man," he requested.

"That will be my assignment," Bud insisted. He wriggled into one of the escape suits and picked up the cutting torch in his pantograph hands. Tom saluted his friend and ushered him into the compression chamber.

A few minutes later Bud was on the sloping bottom, walking cautiously toward the cable net. In another few moments flames shot to the tip of the cutter and Bud nipped through the heavy wire as easily as if it had been a spider web.

He returned to the *Sea Dart,* doffed his Fat Man, and took his station in the window of the bow.

"Okay, Tom, I guess we can proceed."

Tom moved slowly ahead, clearing the sunken net skillfully. Once through, he halted his craft again. The transducer detected the *Devilfish* not far ahead of them.

"That's all I have to know," Tom remarked. "They do have an underwater and underground hide-out. I'm going to come up a bit and raise the periscope to take one quick look at this!"

When the periscope barely cleared the surface, Tom saw the *Devilfish* directly ahead. Where the channel made a sharp turn, the pirates' submarine was neatly hidden in a large cave. Two men had hopped ashore and were racing in the direction of the jetmarine.

The inventor quickly lowered the periscope and told Bud what he had seen.

"I don't think they spotted us," Tom said, making ready to go, "but we're taking no chances."

"Why don't we cut through the channel?" Bud suggested.

"Too big a risk," Tom replied. "They've probably mined the other end of it."

He proposed that they head back in the direction from which they had come and investigate the shore of the island.

"Okay," said Bud. "Let's look for a likely landing spot."

"Then we can reconnoiter the gang's layout from land," Tom added.

He maneuvered his submarine around and had just started forward when the periscope suddenly collapsed. At the same time the *Sea Dart* came to a jarring halt.

"Tom!" Bud shouted. "We're trapped!"

CHAPTER 23

SEA RAIDERS' HIDE-OUT

DESPITE Bud's terrifying announcement Tom continued to blow ballast in an effort to surface the jet-marine. But whatever had descended upon it, Tom realized, was holding the submarine fast near the floor of the channel.

"Are you giving her all the power she's got, Tom?" Bud asked feverishly.

Tom nodded and pointed to the gauge. The engines were overheating, so great was the power being generated in the atomic pile. But the only result was a sickening shudder as muddy water swirled about the trapped submarine.

"What happened to us?" Bud cried out.

"I have an idea," Tom replied, "that Dansitt dropped a gigantic link net on top of us."

"We've got to get out of here!" Bud exclaimed, his eyes on the thermometer. The red marker had risen past the danger point.

Tom quickly shut off the power. He and Bud might be suffocated by the heat, and there was also great danger that the craft itself would explode.

"We can't even send a message out of here on our radio," Bud moaned.

As he said this, there came a faint tapping on the hull of the *Sea Dart*. Tom listened carefully.

"International code," he said, and both boys' lips began to move.

The message was from Dansitt. Figuring it out letter by letter, they translated it:

"You are helpless, Tom Swift. We had this steel net designed especially to catch anyone who got past the mines. It will hold you at the bottom until you agree to surrender. When we lift the net, you will surface and come out of the hatch with your hands up. One false move and we will set off an explosion that will blow you and your sub out of the water."

Bud looked discouraged. "What's the verdict, Tom?"

"There's no choice. We couldn't even escape in the Fat Men with a steel net around us. By the time we might cut through it, Dansitt would capture us."

"Then you'll surrender?"

Tom nodded. "Perhaps we can outwit them once we're topside."

"I'm with you!"

Tom took a wrench and tapped out a return message on the side of the jetmarine.

"We surrender."

While the net was being lifted from the jetmarine,

Tom said he was sure they would be searched—at least partially.

"I don't want the pirates to get hold of my two special pocket pencils—the soldering iron and the two-way radio," he said. "Suppose you hide the radio in one of your shoes, Bud, and I'll put the iron in mine. Even if we limp a little, it may not be noticed."

The transfer was made quickly. Then Tom surfaced the jetmarine, threw open the hatch and climbed out, his hands in the air. Bud followed. Alongside the jetmarine was a launch containing Dansitt and three other men, whom the young pirate identified as Wesman, Chilcote, and Jennig. Wesman took charge of the submarine.

"So you're our prisoners!" Dansitt gloated. "And you'll wish our men had never been captured. Funny how the false rumor got around that Tom Swift was a genius!" he added sarcastically.

As he ordered Tom and Bud into the boat, Jennig, portly and unctuous, pointed to Chilcote and said, "Here's the real genius!"

"Never mind that," Tom said. "Where are my father and Mr. Foster?"

"You'd like to know, wouldn't you?" Dansitt sneered. "Well, when you're locked up, maybe we'll tell you."

After Tom and Bud were seated in the craft, Chilcote snapped handcuffs on them. Jennig started the motor and proceeded toward shore

When they were a few feet from land, Chilcote

pulled an odd-looking key from his pocket. When Bud saw it, his jaw dropped. "An electronic key!" he cried involuntarily.

The scientist smiled. "I always regarded this special electronic key as a fine invention of Tom Swift's," he said. "That's why I borrowed the idea. Despite your careful screening, one of my spies got a job at your plant and stayed just long enough to copy the design for me."

The other two pirates laughed uproariously and Dansitt said, "We borrow lots of things from Tom Swift, don't we, Chilcote? He's even going to lend us his jetmarine!"

Tom's face grew red as the men guffawed.

Bud gritted his teeth and muttered to Tom, "I'd like to take a good crack at them!"

"Keep calm," Tom whispered, as Chilcote beamed the electronic key on what seemed to be a large boulder standing on end at the edge of the hilly beach.

It proved to be a camouflaged door and immediately slid open, revealing the watery entrance to a cave. As the boat glided through the opening, the door closed behind them. Presently an immense, well-lighted cavern loomed ahead.

To one side was a large dock, to which Jennig steered the boat. When Dansitt had made it fast, the two boys were shoved ashore and led through a stout, steel door into a modern, gleaming laboratory.

Tom and Bud could not restrain gasps of amazement when they saw the array of up-to-date equipment, complete in every detail. Who would guess that under a small Caribbean island lay such a formidable scientific installation!

Chilcote pointed toward a bench along one wall. "Sit down," he ordered, then turned and whispered to Dansitt who hurried out.

After a few minutes Dansitt returned. He nodded to Chilcote. "Okay," he said, "I've looked over the jetmarine."

"How does she compare with our new two-man sub?" Chilcote asked quickly.

"Ours is not so completely equipped."

Tom's pulse beat faster. So that was what the pirates were stealing uranium for—to build an atomic submarine of their own!

"Maybe Tom Swift, the great know-it-all, can help you finish your sub, Chilcote," Dansitt sneered.

Tom remained grimly silent. The last thing in the world he intended to do was aid these ruthless men in any way toward furthering their evil plans!

"A good idea," Chilcote said. "But we'll postpone it until after our next raid."

"Okay," said Dansitt.

Tom was curious about the diabolic way these men were flaunting the maritime law. "You can't get away with this much longer," he warned them. "The United States Navy is on your trail."

Dansitt grimaced. "The Navy will never catch up with us!" Then he added, "I'll even let you in on this next job. The *Falcon* is steaming north not far from here. She's carrying a fortune in diamonds in her safe."

As he was saying this, Jennig frowned and Tom noticed that the lawyer was apprehensive.

"Don't you think we'd better clear out right away?" Jennig said. "Maybe we're trying to stretch our luck too far letting just Wesman raid that safe."

Dansitt gestured with his hands. "How can we lose? We're already using Tom Swift's plane and we'll take the jetmarine on this job!"

So Chilcote was piloting Tom's stolen jet! And he had rigged a pulsator in it! Now they were going to use his submarine, too, in their criminal work.

Dansitt ordered the boys to get up and the three pirates roughly pushed them along until they came to a heavy barred aluminum door. Jennig opened it. Tom and Bud were shoved inside and their handcuffs removed. Then the door was closed. Jennig locked it and pocketed his bunch of keys.

"You'll find this cell air-conditioned," Dansitt remarked, "and very comfortable. But let me warn you. Don't touch this door. It's heavily charged with electricity. Touch it and you'll fry!"

The men strode off down the corridor. The boys could overhear Dansitt and Chilcote warning Jennig to keep careful watch of the prisoners while the others were off on the raid.

As Tom paced around the cell, which was merely a cave hewn out of the rocks, he observed that the door was insulated from the frame and the earthen floor. Suspecting from this that Dansitt's threat was correct, he decided to try proving it.

The inventor removed his belt, and holding the

leather, swung the metal buckle to make contact between the door and the frame. There was a blinding bright blue flash of light from the hissing electric arc formed by the contact, and the buckle bounced back, melted out of shape.

"Dansitt wasn't fooling," Tom said grimly.

He realized that if he and Bud were to escape it would have to be by a clever ruse. He began to think fast.

CHAPTER 24

A TRICKY INVENTION

BEFORE TOM had a chance to plan any strategy, Jennig returned and once more warned the boys about the electrified cell door.

"I don't want anything to happen to you while I'm in charge," he said apprehensively. "Chilcote can do what he pleases when he gets back."

Tom detected the slight hint of nervousness in Jennig's manner. Perhaps the wily lawyer did not relish his lone role as guard. If the man had any fears about his part in the pirate enterprise, Tom determined to encourage them and possibly weaken the man's allegiance to Dansitt and Chilcote.

"Mr. Jennig," he said, "you may be shrewd on legal angles, but you're obviously on the losing end in this pirate deal."

"What are you getting at, Swift?" the other retorted, eying the youth suspiciously. "A double cross? Nonsense! I know when I'm well fixed."

"You think you are," Tom replied coolly. "But don't forget your pals have my jet and sub."

"What of it?" asked Jennig with a scowl.

Tom pursued his point quickly. "Dansitt and Chilcote realize the United States authorities have found out their method of attack and are hot on their trail. So—"

"Don't hand me that stuff," Jennig interrupted, giving a harsh laugh. "We've got those authorities completely bamboozled!"

Tom looked the lawyer straight in the eye. "Maybe your two cronies aren't as sure of that, though. They could easily make their getaway in my plane and sub with the haul of diamonds—including your share—and leave you in the lurch here."

As Jennig glared at him, Tom continued:

"Then, while they're safe in some new hide-out, you'll have to take the punishment for the robberies and kidnapings all by yourself."

"You're crazy!" shrilled Jennig. "Dansitt and Chilcote need me. They'd be in a fine pickle if I—"

"You mean," Tom broke in, leading him on, "if you weren't along to get them out of trouble?"

"Sure." The lawyer's voice rose. "They'd have been nabbed long ago if I hadn't been around. I've got enough on those two—"

He stopped abruptly, aware that he was admitting too much, and said smoothly:

"Don't concern yourself about my welfare, Swift. Better start worrying about your own."

Tom shrugged. "Oh, I'm not concerned at all," he replied blandly. "Just curious as to why you insist on being a dupe for Dansitt and Chilcote."

The boys were certain that this time Tom's needling took effect. Jennig's heavy face turned a dark red, but he made no reply. Did his silence mean that he suddenly did not know how to answer?

Tom hurled another idea at him. "Look, Jennig, this is your chance to outwit Dansitt. Set Bud and me free and we'll help you intercept him in the *Devilfish*."

For a moment Jennig seemed to be considering Tom's unexpected proposition. The next minute, though, he uttered his raucous laugh.

"That's rich!" he said. "An easy way to turn me in, all right! No thanks, Swift. I'm not taking your bait!"

With a derisive snort he strutted off down the corridor.

"Nice try, Tom," Bud remarked. "Maybe you planted a few seeds of distrust in his mind about Dansitt and Company."

"If so, let's hope some of them take root," Tom said. "In the meantime, we'd better work out another plan for getting out of here and quick!"

"Maybe your Uncle Ned could help if you could contact him," Bud suggested.

"Boy, am I getting fogbound!" Tom exclaimed. "Let's have my pencil transmitter."

Bud removed the miniature set from his shoe and Tom tuned it. At first there was no response but finally a voice said:

"Yes?"

Tom, wary about revealing his identity for fear the pirates had Ned Newton's set, replied:

"Let me identify your voice."

"Tom!" the other voice exclaimed in muffled tones. "Where are you?"

"Dad!" Am I glad to hear from you! Bud and I are prisoners on Spaniel Island. Are you here too?"

"Yes. I'm in a cell with Ned and Jim Foster. The pirates took everything away from us but this transmitter so we haven't been able to escape."

He reported that all of them were in good condition physically but had just about given up hope of being rescued. Mr. Newton took the set and told Tom that he and the others were being held in a cell far down the corridor.

"Why wouldn't you let us contact you?" Tom asked.

"I was afraid the pirates would learn about it," he replied. "Then harm would have come to you as well as me. The gang had several raids scheduled for the next eight days. After that, they were going to decide about me. This could have been my last day on earth."

"But it's not going to be," Tom said. "Is your door electrically charged like ours?"

"No, Tom. Try to short-circuit the electric current in yours. Then you can figure a way to get out."

"Probably Jennig will return and I can get the keys," he replied.

Tom's heart pounded with excitement. "Uncle

Ned," he said as a sudden thought struck him, "I believe I can do it!"

"If you can, you may short-circuit the dynamo and
put out all the lights," Uncle Ned remarked.

"How will you accomplish the short-circuiting,
Tom?" Bud asked, as the inventor signed off. "Not
with your belt buckle?"

Tom knew that with the high charge on the door
he would need something much heavier than the
buckle to accomplish the short circuit. He pulled
the soldering-iron pencil from his shoe.

"I think that by using the heat I can generate in
the end of this pencil," he said, "I can melt enough
of the metal in the door to cause it to run down and
touch the floor."

"Making the short circuit between the door and
the floor," Bud remarked.

"Right."

Tom realized he might accidentally touch the
door while working, and looked about for something to insulate him from the floor. A heavy wooden
bench stood against one wall of the cell. This was
perfect for his purpose.

Dragging the bench over to the door he knelt on
it, reached down, and clicked on the pencil. When
the tip was hot, he applied it against the bottom of
one of the bars. Slowly the metal began to melt and
run down toward the insulation. Just as the flowing
metal neared the floor, Tom, anticipating a sudden
flash, turned his head and warned Bud to do the
same.

As the metal touched the floor there was a sharp sputtering, a blinding flash, then darkness. Tom had completed the short circuit! The door was no longer a menace!

"You must have blown out the main generator!" Bud whispered gleefully, then added, "Listen!"

The boys could hear heavy footsteps in the corridor.

"It's probably Jennig," Bud remarked. "No doubt he thinks we touched the door and were electrocuted!"

"Let's pretend we were, then try to nab him and get the key," Tom proposed.

Jennig's steps became slow as he felt his way toward the cell. Then he retreated.

"Good night!" Bud said. "He's leaving. Maybe he'll throw over the circuit breaker!"

"He can't put the charge back in the door until the weld I made is broken," Tom replied. "I think he's gone for a flashlight."

The young inventor's surmise was correct. A moment later the man came back, beaming a light before him. Tom and Bud flattened themselves on the floor of the cell on either side of the door. Jennig beamed his light inside and peered at the boys.

As he gave a grunt of astonishment Tom and Bud sprang upward, reached through the bars, and grasped the lawyer by the shirt front. Jennig squealed in horrified amazement and tried to break loose.

But Bud held him in a viselike grip, while Tom

took the flashlight and then removed the keys from Jennig's pocket. Quickly the young inventor took his soldering pencil and cut through the newly made strip of metal.

Tom, then, tried various keys. Finding the right one, he opened the door. Bud pushed Jennig inside the cell and Tom locked the door.

"You can't do this! Let me out of here!" the man yelled.

Bud held him in a viselike grip

The boys did not even bother to answer. Tom said, "Wait here, Bud, while I find the generator. I'll make sure everything's safe, then throw the circuit breaker."

Tom hurried off. In five minutes the underground hide-out was flooded with light.

Next, Tom and Bud combed the place and made certain it was free of pirates. Then they went to release the prisoners.

"Tom! Bud!" the men cried.

They slapped the boys on the back and wrung their hands.

A deluge of questions was on everyone's lips but thoughts of capturing the pirates came first. Tom led the way to Chilcote's laboratory. There he tuned in a radio receiver over which he hoped to hear Chilcote and Dansitt reporting progress on the raid. A moment later the older scientist's authoritative voice came through. "I'm starting my blackout, Dansitt. Here goes!"

A minute later he repeated it. "I'm starting the blackout again, Sidney. The first didn't seem to work."

Presently Dansitt's voice reported, "It didn't work again. I'm looking through my periscope. People on deck are standing up. Try again."

The group in the underground laboratory stared questioningly at one another. What was going on? Was the pulsator broken?

Suddenly Tom exclaimed, "I know what it is! Bud, we didn't shut off the distorter on the *Sea Dart!* But Dansitt doesn't realize that!"

"You mean Chilcote *can't* black out the people on the freighter?" Uncle Ned cried.

"Exactly."

Suddenly a string of expletives came over the loud-speaker and Tom quickly shut it off.

"They'll probably be back here right away," he stated. "We must work fast."

"We'll be ready for them," Bud said.

"Right. Chilcote will be here first. Come on, let's go topside," Tom suggested.

Uncle Ned, who had seen more of the pirates' hide-out than the others, led them through a passageway and out into the sunlight of the island. Everyone took deep breaths of fresh air, then Tom explained a plan for the capture.

"Bud and I will cross over the channel to the airstrip and intercept Chilcote."

"Yes." Bud grinned. "That pirate's going to need a really big black patch on his eye when I get through with him!"

He spied a rowboat on the other side of the channel and offered to get it.

"Just call me a Labrador retriever," he said, dashing to the water.

He took off his shoes and swam to the other side. Five minutes later he was back with the rowboat. Tom advised the others to hide in a fisherman's shack which stood nearby. When they were out of sight, he and Bud stepped into the boat and rowed to the opposite shore. There they hid among some scrubby bushes.

"I wonder how long we'll have to wait," Bud said impatiently.

"No time at all," Tom replied. "I think I hear my jet."

With an eerie whistle Tom's stolen craft whipped across the island.

"He'll come in for a landing now," Bud replied.

"I hope he doesn't have any suspicions that we're no longer prisoners."

Suddenly a queer expression came over Bud's face. "Tom, I feel—"

"The same with me," Tom remarked. "I'm—spinning—"

His voice trailed off as he felt a paralysis spreading rapidly through his limbs. His vision blurred and his head reeled. What had happened?

Dimly he was aware of Bud pitching to the ground. Then Tom knew the answer: Chilcote had fired on them with the pulsator!

The next second all was blackness!

CHAPTER 25

VICTORY

HOW LONG Tom lay unconscious he did not know. But when he opened his eyes he noticed that Bud also was stirring. Tom's head felt as if it had been hit by a sledge hammer, but gradually the intense pain subsided and he sat up. Bud tried to struggle to his feet.

"What—what hit us?" he asked, still dazed.

When Tom said he thought it had been the pulsator on his stolen jet plane, Bud looked worried.

"It probably knocked out the others, too," he said. "We'd better find out."

But as the boys stood up they heard shouts. Mr. Swift, Uncle Ned, and Mr. Foster were signaling from across the channel.

"Thank goodness you're all right," Tom cried. "Were you blacked out?"

"Blacked out?" Uncle Ned queried. "No. We came to see what happened to Chilcote."

"He's still over here?" Tom asked in surprise.

"You mean you don't know he crashed?" Mr. Foster exclaimed, amazed.

Tom explained that he and Bud had been blacked out, then said they would look for Chilcote. Mr. Foster pointed out the direction where the plane had gone down and the boys hurried across the marshy shore front to where Tom's stolen jet lay, half in the water and half on land.

While coming in for a landing on the sandy runway, the plane apparently had swerved off the beach. The jet upended and flipped over on its back.

"What could have gone wrong?" Bud asked.

Tom thought that perhaps the pulsator had been jarred loose from its safety catch and had swung around on its pivot, knocking the pirate unconscious.

Reaching the damaged plane, Tom forced open the door. Chilcote lay face down, unconscious. The boys lifted him onto the sandy shore.

"The pulsator was put out of commission in the crash," Bud said. "And a good thing, too."

Tom quickly examined Chilcote but could find no injuries except a bump on his forehead. In a few minutes the man revived and looked around. Seeing his captors, the scientist grew sullen and cursed his ill fortune.

The boys rowed him across the channel. He was put into one of the vacant cells and Mr. Foster said he would remain on guard.

"Now for Dansitt," Bud said grimly.

He and Tom made their way with Mr. Swift and Ned Newton to the beach and scanned the ocean with binoculars they had picked up in Chilcote's laboratory.

"The *Sea Dart* ought to be here soon," said Tom. Minutes went by, then suddenly he shouted, "I see something!"

With hands cupped over their eyes to shade them from the glare of the sun, the group looked eagerly out to sea.

"I can see it too!" Bud shouted. "Yes, it's our sub!"

Quickly the group hid behind a dune so that they would not be seen through the extended periscope of the submarine. Tom smiled as the craft headed directly toward the channel. A moment later the jet-marine began to submerge.

"Where is the best spot to grab those two in the jetmarine?" Bud asked.

As the others debated where the best place might be, Bud took the glasses and trained them on the water.

"Look out there!" he cried. "There are two objects way out on the water. They look like our Fat Men."

Tom took the binoculars and pressed them to his eyes. What he saw made his heart sink. The two Fat Men were indeed bobbing on the surface of the sea.

"That means the *Sea Dart* has gone to the bottom!" he groaned.

Bud's face was livid with anger. "When I get my hands on that pair—"

"Come on, Bud," Tom urged. "Let's go pick up the Fat Men."

The two boys raced to the rowboat, jumped in, and rowed toward the spot where the pirates were bobbing about. He tapped on the metal shell of each escape suit and got a response from inside.

"Take them in tow, Bud, while I man the oars," Tom directed.

Reaching out, his friend grasped the two figures and tied them to the stern of the boat. Then he scrambled to the seat beside Tom and they returned to shore. Landing, the boys pulled the Fat Men up on the beach. Dansitt and Wesman emerged and were immediately made prisoners. The last two of the pirate gang had been captured!

Dansitt tried to make a break for it, but Bud sent the sallow youth sprawling headfirst into the pebbles on the beach.

"All right," Dansitt said as he arose and brushed the sand out of his hair, "you may have us, but that wonderful sub of yours, Tom Swift, is sunk and in deep water too. You'll never raise it."

"Don't be too sure of that!" Tom said. Turning to his father, he added, "We can raise the *Sea Dart* with that giant electromagnet you invented several years ago, Dad. Don't you think so?"

"Yes, I believe we can, Tom. Radio Hanson to bring it down here in the *Sky Queen* and we'll go to work at once."

While the others marched the two pirates off to an underground cell, the young inventor hurried to the radio in Chilcote's laboratory. Quickly contacting Hanson in Shopton, he first told of the pirates' capture.

"Tom, that's magnificent!" cried the engineer unbelievingly. "I'll report this to Admiral Hopkins immediately."

Tom then reported that the jetmarine had been sunk and requested that the giant magnet be flown to Spaniel Island.

"I'll start preparations right away," Hanson promised. "We should reach you by afternoon."

While the group waited for the magnet's arrival, they quizzed their three prisoners. At first Chilcote and Dansitt refused to talk, but Wesman, hoping for a light sentence, turned state's evidence. First he told why the *Sea Dart* had sunk.

"Dansitt wanted to run it but he didn't know how," Wesman said. "He pressed the wrong lever and we hit the bottom nosefirst. Got stuck in the mud. Then Bright Boy here decided we'd better use the escape suits. He left the inner and outer hatches of the compression chamber of your sub open and flooded the interior."

"Shut up!" Dansitt cried, glaring at his companion.

"Why should I?" the older man snapped. "You and Chilcote were going to make us all wealthy. Instead, we're going to jail."

He revealed that Chilcote had organized the pirates. Wesman had joined as an expert submarine pilot, while Dansitt played the part of a spy. Jennig, a long-time friend of Chilcote, had been induced to handle legal matters for the group at such a fantastic figure that he was willing to jeopardize his career.

Chilcote had figured out the strange coin as a means of identifying members of the group who were not known to one another. Since it was dangerous for Tom to be in possession of the secret coin, Dansitt had gone to the Swift home to retrieve the one he had dropped on the airfield.

"Sid's father is going to be heartbroken when he finds out his son's a thief," Wesman went on. "Why, that kid even planned the raid on a McIntosh and Dansitt ship."

"Was that to throw me off his trail?" Tom asked.

"Yes. And he thought up the idea of saying Mr. Swift had been taken to the North Woods to get you out of the Caribbean."

When the conference was over, the boys investigated the kitchen of the pirates' hide-out. There was little food but several cans of soup. Just as they finished eating, a body of government officials arrived by plane. They at once confiscated the two pirate submarines and investigated the hide-out. Then, after congratulating Tom and his group on their fine work in rounding up the pirates, they took all the prisoners away with them.

Directly afterward, the *Sky Queen* was seen hovering over the island. Contacting it by radio, Tom told Hanson he would like to start work at once.

"Okay. Give me directions where to lower the magnet," the engineer said.

Tom and Bud got into the Fat Men, turned on

their activators, and propelled themselves over the surface of the water to the spot where they had seen the *Sea Dart* go down. Submerging, they located the sunken submarine and Tom signaled for the magnet to be lowered.

The giant disk came down on its cables, directly midships. The boys, maneuvering their pantograph arms, placed the magnet in position, then surfaced.

"Okay," Tom radioed, wondering if the experiment would work.

Hanson flicked a switch sending electric power into the magnet. Then the jet lifters of the *Sky Queen* roared out power as the cables pulled the jetmarine slowly off the ocean floor and above the surface of the water. As it hung in mid-air, water pouring out from the flooded hull, Bud cried over his transmitter:

"Thar she blows, jetmariner!"

After the *Sea Dart* had been brought to shore, the job of completely draining and drying the interior of the submarine began. But this was soon accomplished with pumps and air compressors. When Tom examined the machinery, he found to his delight that none of it had been damaged by its brief contact with the sea water.

"We cheated Dansitt out of that pleasure!" he remarked to Bud after a successful test run.

Meanwhile, the *Sky Queen* had landed on the island. As soon as the boys had made the jetmarine secure in her temporary berth, they walked over to the mammoth Flying Lab. A familiar figure appeared in the open doorway high above the ground. He was wearing a makeshift costume that made him look like an old-time pirate.

"Chow!" Tom yelled, and everyone burst into laughter.

"Jest thought I'd have to help you celebrate

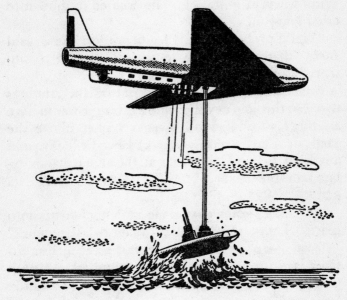

The cables slowly raised the jetmarine off the ocean floor

proper," he said. "I got a real pirate meal waitin' for you."

"What is it?" Bud asked. "Skull and crossbone stew?"

The meal proved to be a fine fish dinner. During

it plans were made for leaving Spaniel Island. Mr. Foster had already sent a radio message for his yacht and would return to Florida in it.

Tom's stolen plane would be repaired speedily in the Lab's workshop and Bud would fly it home. Mr. Swift and Tom would take the jetmarine to the States where Admiral Hopkins wanted to show it to other Navy men.

"You'll probably get such a big order, Tom," said Bud, "that you'll have to put off that trip into space."

But Tom did not intend to put off the fabulous trip. On this journey the young inventor was to have adventures and narrow escapes higher above the earth than any scientist ever had been—far beyond anything he could imagine at the moment—as related in the next volume, **TOM SWIFT AND HIS ROCKET SHIP.**

"Nothing's going to stop me from my journey into space," Tom replied to Bud. "Want to come along?"

"Can you promise me a few pirates and a ripsnorting adventure like this last one?" Bud asked with a grin. "If not, I think I'll stick to the ocean and the *Sea Dart!*"

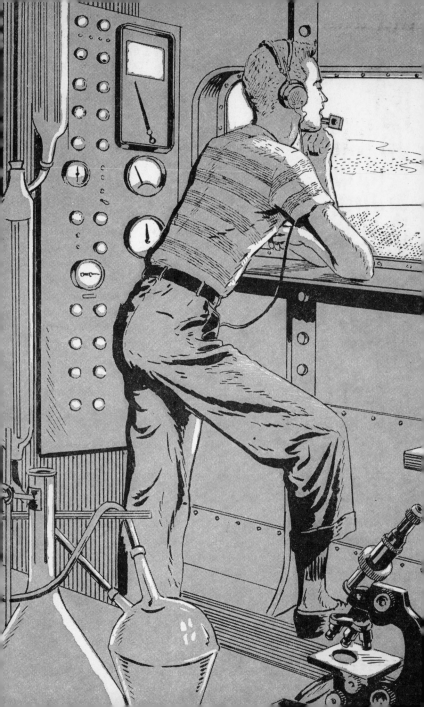